ALSO BY MELISSA DE LA CRUZ

A DESCENDANTS NOVEL

#1 *NEW YORK TIMES* BEST-SELLING AUTHOR
MELISSA DE LA CRUZ

BASED ON *DESCENDANTS 2* WRITTEN BY
SARA PARRIOTT &
JOSANN MCGIBBON

𝒟isnℯᴩ • HYPERION
LOS ANGELES   NEW YORK

First Edition, May 2017
10 9 8 7 6 5 4 3 2 1
FAC-020093-17097

Printed in the United States of America

This book is set in Adobe Caslon, Adobe Caslon Pro/Monotype;
Albyona English No. 1/SIAS; Harlean/Laura Worthington;
Linger On/Gustav & Brun
Designed by Marci Senders

Library of Congress Cataloging-in-Publication Control Number:
2017008125

ISBN 978-1-4847-8128-9

Reinforced binding

Visit www.DisneyBooks.com
and www.DisneyDescendants.com

SUSTAINABLE FORESTRY INITIATIVE
Certified Sourcing
www.sfiprogram.org
SFI-00993

THIS LABEL APPLIES TO TEXT STOCK

For Mattie & Mike,
Always

And for

Heidi, Sasha, and Calista Madzar,

friends & allies, thank you for all your support
and enthusiasm for the series!

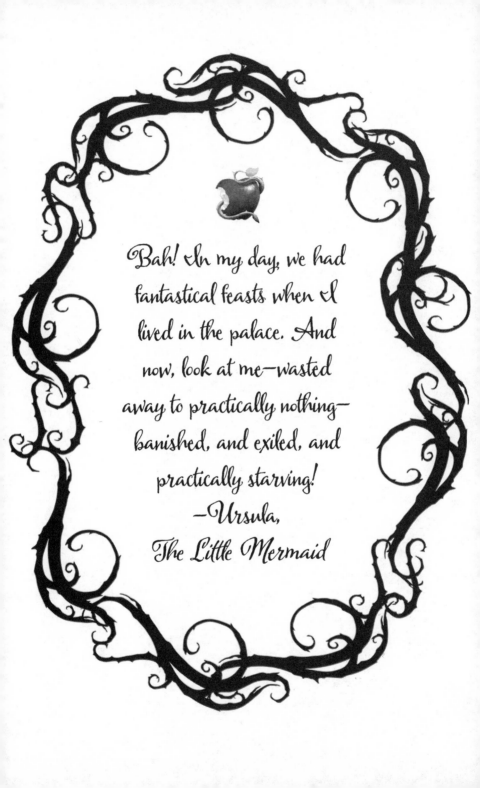

Bah! In my day, we had
fantastical feasts when I
lived in the palace. And
now, look at me—wasted
away to practically nothing—
banished, and exiled, and
practically starving!
—Ursula,
The Little Mermaid

Left Behind

O nce upon a time, the offspring of an evil fairy and a sea witch were friends. Mal, daughter of Maleficent, Mistress of Darkness, and Uma, daughter of Ursula, Witch of the Seas, were an inseparable duo, partners-in-petty-crime. Mal had purple hair, flashing green eyes, and a mischievous streak, while Uma had turquoise locks, eyes the color of the abyss, and a wicked sense of fun. Luckily for the poor, unfortunate souls who lived on the Isle of the Lost, they didn't get to see each other very much, since they lived on opposite sides of the island and went to rival schools—Dragon Hall for Mal and Serpent Prep for Uma.

Life on the Isle of the Lost—where all the villain folk

had been banished after King Beast united all the good kingdoms and exiled all the evildoers and their snarky sidekicks—was already difficult. For one, an impenetrable dome covered the island and its surrounding waters, keeping out any source of magic, as well as every kind of Wi-Fi network. For another, most of the island's residents subsisted on leftovers from Auradon's mainland along with the goblins' terrible coffee. But life always got a little worse during the summer when school was out, because that was when Mal and Uma could hit the streets together again.

They would rampage up and down the island, terrorizing step-granddaughters and traumatizing even the most stalwart goons, and no one would dare voice a peep of annoyance, for fear of something truly frightening—*the girls' mothers.*

One hot day in June, not long after each had turned ten, Mal and Uma were playing on the docks by the water. The two bad little girls were pranking Hook's crew, making tick-tock noises to scare the pirate captain himself, and getting on Smee's already agitated nerves. They giggled naughtily behind some empty barrels as their best trick of all went off without a hitch. One pirate after another tripped and fell on the slippery wooden planks, which they had covered with a nearly invisible slime. It was Mal's idea to coat the decks with bilge and oily, murky scum, and she laughed with glee to see it work so well.

"Here comes Cruella De Vil," said Mal, spotting a telltale

black-and-white bouffant rising from the crowd of pirates. "Let's get her!"

Cruella was a nemesis of theirs. As one of the only citizens on the Isle who wasn't afraid of Maleficent or Ursula, the Dalmatian-obsessed lady never hesitated to pinch their ears when they tried to make her their victim. They were determined to get her back one of these days, but they'd have to be crafty.

They watched her sauntering down the docks with a ratty spotted fur on her shoulder, glaring at everyone she met.

"What's she doing down here, anyway?" whispered Uma.

"Goblin barge is arriving soon, and she likes to have first dibs," explained Mal, holding her breath as Cruella sashayed closer and closer to where they were hiding. "She's always hoping someone's thrown away an old fur coat."

The girls looked at each other, eyes sparkling with mischief. Mal raced to pour another batch of the disgusting concoction in Cruella's path, but the giant bucket was too heavy for her.

"Hurry!" said Uma, running to grab the bucket's other handle.

"I've got it!" said Mal.

"Let me!" said Uma. "You did Gaston!"

Mal chuckled darkly at the memory of the big man going bottoms-up on the dock and finally crashing over the railing with a loud roar and splash, his sons slack-jawed at the sight.

Uma pulled the bucket to her side.

"Stop it! Let go!" Mal demanded.

"*You* let go! You're splashing it on me!" whined Uma.

They each yanked on the bucket. As Uma wrenched it away, Mal lost her grip on the handle, overturning the pail and its contents—and she tripped and fell upon their own slippery puddle.

"Mal!" yelped Uma, as her friend skittered down the length of the dock, flailing, all the way to the edge.

"Help! Help me!" Mal screamed, as she attempted to grasp the wooden rails while she sped toward the sea. "I can't swim!"

But the irony that the mastermind had been caught in her own naughty little prank and the sight of her purple friend sliding down the docks like a flopping wet fish was too hilarious for Uma to resist, and instead of running to help, the little sea witch was doubled up on her knees in laughter.

Mal spun down past the gaggle of pirates, past a confused Cruella De Vil, and disappeared overboard.

That shook Uma from her laughing fit. "Mal!" she called, rushing to the railing's edge. "Mal! Where are you? Are you okay?" Uma craned her neck, searching the churning waters for a sign of her friend.

Her heart stopped, for she couldn't catch sight of Mal's purple head anywhere in the waves, and while Maleficent might find it amusing that her daughter had landed in the drink, she would not take too kindly to the news that her one and only spawn was gone forever.

"Mal! Where are you?" Uma cried, a little desperately now.

Uma felt a tap on her shoulder and looked up to see Mal standing there, totally dry. "You didn't fall in!" she cried in relief.

"I caught a wooden rung right before I fell," said Mal sweetly.

"You're all right!"

"Yes, I'm okay," said Mal with a sugary smile that suddenly turned evil. "But you're not!" she yelled, and before Uma could blink, Mal reached behind her back and dumped a huge bucket of smelly and disgusting baby shrimps all over Uma's head. Turned out Mal had scampered back up on the docks just in time to see the goblins unloading the latest catch from the barge. Furious at her friend for laughing at her bad luck, Mal decided to create a little bad luck herself.

Uma screamed.

And screamed.

And screamed.

Sadly, the smell never quite left Uma's hair, no matter how many times she washed it.

Much worse, Mal's nickname for her caught on, and from that fateful day forward, everyone called Uma "Shrimpy" behind her back.

Except for Mal, of course, who called Uma Shrimpy *to her face.*

From the sandbox to the doomball courts, the animosity between the two girls festered and bubbled over the years—especially during rival *super-sinister-thirteen* birthday parties, which they scheduled on the same night. Somehow, Mal always ended up on top.

But Uma knew the day would come when she would beat Mal at her own game.

One fine day . . .

Three years later, that day had not yet come. Especially not after the shiny black limousine drove up to the Isle of the Lost. Uma had never seen a car like that—the only means of transportation on the island were rickshaws pulled by goblins, old skateboards, and rusty bikes. It was clear limousines were more than just cars; they were moving cocoons of luxury, decked out in buttery leather seats and filled to the brim with sugary drinks and snacks.

So what was it doing here of all places, on this forgotten island of villains?

The young sea witch elbowed her way to the front of the gaping crowd so she could get a better look at what was happening. At sixteen she was small for her age, but more than made up for it by cutting a striking figure. She wore her turquoise hair in a river of long braids that fell down her back, and was partial to patchwork leather dresses and low boots decorated with fishing nets and seashells. Truly, Uma was one of the head-turners on the island, not that she cared. Uma had bigger fish to fry—literally, since she worked at her mom's Fish and Chips Shoppe.

The assembled group of louts, toughs, and goons (otherwise known as the population of the island) were *ooh*ing and *ahh*ing at the sight of the marvelous automobile. No one had any idea why it was there, or what it meant, but before a riot broke out among the villainous ranks, the door to Maleficent's castle opened and Evie, Carlos, and Jay walked out carrying luggage, followed by their parents.

"Bring home the gold!" yelled Jafar.

"Bring home a puppy!" urged Cruella De Vil.

"Bring home a prince!" Evil Queen cried.

Uma nudged the fellow on the left. "What's going on?" she asked. "Are they leaving?"

The henchman nodded, barely concealed envy on his face. "Rumor has it they're going to Auradon."

"Auradon? Why?" said Uma, appalled and intrigued at the same time.

"To go to school. Some kind of new proclamation or something. They've been chosen to attend Auradon Prep."

Carlos, Jay, and Evie trooped into the car.

"Is anyone else going?" Uma asked, just as a fourth

villain kid burst through the castle doors. An annoyed-looking Mal handed her backpack to the driver.

Of course Mal had been chosen too.

Uma watched as Mal looked up to the balcony, where Maleficent raised her staff in goodbye, her green eyes blazing. After a moment, Mal's purple head disappeared into the limousine as well.

Somehow, instead of feeling glee at the sight of the four villain kids' depressed and resentful faces, Uma only felt a spark . . . of envy.

Why wasn't *she* chosen to leave the Isle of the Lost and live in Auradon? Was she not wicked enough? Not special enough? Why was she left behind like a common goblin?

And why was Mal chosen instead?

Uma had to find a way out of the Isle of the Lost. If Mal and her crew were living in Auradon, then *that* was the place to be—the place where *Uma* needed to be. Not here, working day in and day out at Ursula's Fish and Chips Shoppe slinging fish cakes and lost-soul casseroles to the rabble. Uma was special: she was the sea witch's daughter, a force to be reckoned with! She couldn't stay here, lost and unloved and unappreciated!

There was nothing she could do, however. The weeks went by, and the dome was impenetrable. There was no way out of the Isle of the Lost. No matter how much she wanted to leave, there was simply no escape.

Until one day a few months later . . . one ordinary day, like every other, but unlike every one that came before it, when something different happened.

Uma was getting her hair done at her favorite beauty salon, Curl Up & Dye, watching the television while sitting under the dryer.

"It's the Coronation. Wish we could be there," the hairdresser said with a sigh, as a handsome Prince Ben bowed his head to accept the king's crown and the duties that came with it.

"Mmm," said Uma, indifferent to Auradon's pomp and glory. Young Dizzy, the wicked step-granddaughter who was sweeping up tendrils from the floor, was glued to the sight.

On-screen, Fairy Godmother was holding out her wand, but in the blink of an eye, someone else had taken it, and then a huge explosion rocked the whole island.

"What was that?" Uma cried, rushing out of her chair and running outside, just in time to watch a dark shape rising up into the sky, flying like a veritable bat out of hell.

"Magic! The dome is broken!" she heard someone cry. "Maleficent is gone!"

Like the rest of the island's residents, Uma saw her chance—it was time to go! Time to leave the Isle of the Lost forever! But without a bridge, there was only one way to get to the mainland, so the island's residents were scrambling to the shoreline. Uma followed the crowd rushing down to the docks to find a ship, a boat, a way out—and just as she had clambered on the last goblin rowboat and made it a few miles away from shore, the dome closed again.

They ran smack into the invisible wall.

Wha—? How—?

Uma pressed her nose against the unseen barrier and tried not to scream.

She was still stuck on this witch-forsaken rock. Later that day, she watched with a weary annoyance as Mal and her friends celebrated their victory, dancing around some castle while fireworks went off in the distance.

Mal and her crew.

Crew.

That was it! That was how she was going to get off this island. As much as she didn't want to admit it, she couldn't do it alone. What was that saying? *No man is an island?* Well, no one should live on an island either, at least not unless they had a choice in the matter.

In any case, Uma vowed then and there to put together a real crew of her own.

Friends don't let friends stay on the Isle of the Lost.

Under the sea

I admit that in the past
I've been nasty,
They weren't kidding when
they called me, well, a witch,
But you'll find that nowadays,
I've mended all my ways,
Repented, seen the light
and took a switch . . .
—Ursula,
The Little Mermaid

chapter

1

A Celebration of Auradon

"And now, please welcome Sebastian and the Seven Wonders of the Sea!" the cheerful announcer, a merman floating above the waves, joyfully declared. A magnificent clam-shaped stage rose from the ocean and slowly opened to display the famous crab and a row of pretty mermaids launching into a rollicking tune. The sandy beachfront in front of Ariel and Eric's castle had been turned into an outdoor stadium, complete with bleachers above the water. Seated high up in the royal box with Ben and her friends, Mal eagerly clapped with the rest of the audience gathered for the start of the annual Seaside

Festival, a daylong celebration of merfolk life. Next to her, Evie was taking zapps on her phone with Arabella, Ariel's niece, who was something of a fashion maven and idolized Evie's style. The two were currently sporting matching V-braids and poison-heart necklaces. Evie had even made Arabella's outfit, a lavender-colored blouse with a lace bodice along with a distressed leather skirt.

Evie and Arabella couldn't stop giggling. "What's so funny?" Mal asked.

"Mal, do this filter with us!" Evie said, and Mal obliged, sticking her tongue out at the camera. The image on the phone turned the three of them into mermaids complete with curved green tails.

"That's pretty much what I look like when I swim," Arabella said approvingly.

"Cool." Mal smiled.

On the stage, Sebastian was zooming around on his claws, belting his heart out while the mermaids harmonized and splashed, swimming in synchronized patterns around the stage.

"Who knew crustaceans were so talented?" Mal whispered to Ben as Sebastian hit a high note. Ben grinned and squeezed her arm in agreement.

He looked so handsome in his royal coat and sash, the golden crown on his honey-colored hair. The crowd cheered when they saw him smile, and he waved back from the balcony. "Come on, Mal, give them a wave," he urged.

Mal hesitantly raised her hand and waved as well, and another cheer rose from the crowd. She was still getting used to the position of royal girlfriend and all the attention it generated. She never wanted to embarrass Ben, and she was keenly aware of how different she was from his former girlfriend. Audrey was the epitome of an Auradon princess—she looked so perfectly sweet and lovely that birds would perch on her finger, while Mal was definitely a villain kid from the Isle. A reformed villain, for sure, but chirping birds certainly wouldn't be worshipping her any time soon. Unlike Audrey, Mal preferred to wear leather pants rather than pretty dresses. So far the people of Auradon didn't seem to mind, and Mal was grateful they were so accepting.

"How do they fly so high?" asked Carlos, as the mermaids shot into the air to the rhythm of the music and performed dizzying backflips. "I thought they were mermaids, not fairies."

"They're jumping, not flying," said Jay, looking envious. "It's like water parkour."

"Oh, like what they do in R.O.A.R. competitions," Carlos teased, meaning the Royal Order of Auradon Regiment. "You know, all that sword-fighting, flips and stuff, or as you call it, 'jumping.'"

"Right, when are tryouts again?"

"After our last tourney game."

"Cool," said Jay, adjusting his red beanie over his forehead. Mal shushed the guys as the mermaids finished their song and the clam closed again and disappeared under-water. Next, the orchestra was introduced, showcasing a talented variety of sea creatures playing instruments in a custom-built stage-size aquarium. It was a joyful, dazzling celebration. Growing up, Mal recalled watching (okay, sneering at) the festival coverage on Auradon News Network, but that was nothing compared to seeing it live, to marveling at the shimmering scales on the mermaids and watching a killer shark pluck harp strings with its fin so delicately. The Seaside Festival was just the first in an annual all-kingdom "Celebration of Auradon" wherein every kingdom hosted the king with a plethora of festivities that showcased their unique culture.

Suddenly, Mal felt something shift in her pocket and got a glimpse of the Dragon's Egg she had found in the Catacombs of Doom only a few days earlier. The evil talisman had been disarmed, but its surface was crisscrossed with fine green lines, and they were multiplying by the minute.

Mal knew it was dangerous, but she couldn't help keeping the Dragon's Egg with her at all times. It had to be destroyed soon, and Ben kept reminding her about it, but she always had an excuse as to why she couldn't see Fairy Godmother just yet. For some reason, she just wanted to keep the egg a little longer. There was no rush just yet, was there? Besides, the Dragon's Egg was so warm and toasty in her pocket.

"It's nice to be back," said Mal. "Even though we

were only gone for a day, it felt like we were down in the Catacombs for a long time."

Ben nodded. "I'm glad everything worked out."

"Thanks to you," she said, since Ben had appeared at the last minute to set everything right on that adventure.

"And you!" he said, nudging her.

"And us!" chimed in Carlos, Jay, and Evie teasingly.

"Totally! Group hug?" said Mal, opening up her arms.

"Group hug!" they chorused, and the five of them shared an affectionate embrace. Evie pulled in Arabella too, so she wouldn't feel left out, even though she hadn't braved the Catacombs of Doom with them.

The orchestra finished its performance with a roaring crescendo of percussion by a group of manta rays, just as a proud King Triton rose from the waves. He held his golden trident to the sky and the entire coastline exploded in a dazzling canvas of color and light and magic. The crowd thrilled at the sight, and Ben put an arm around Mal as the fireworks boomed all around them. She leaned her head against his chest and nestled into his arms, feeling lucky and content—and just a tiny bit guilty about the Dragon's Egg hidden in her pocket.

After the show, the gang wandered down to the exhibitor booths to shop for Seaside souvenirs before the start of the mer-games. Mal and Ben walked hand in hand behind their friends, lingering at a stand selling seashell necklaces.

"Pretty," said Mal, holding up a particularly luminescent piece, a creamy pastel-colored one polished to a high shine.

"Each one is unique." The mermaid attending the booth smiled. "No two are alike in all the world."

"Do you want one?" asked Ben, reaching for his wallet.

Mal smiled and shook her head. "No, I just like looking at them." She handed the seashell necklace back to the mermaid.

"They're not just beautiful," the mermaid told them. "Each of them contains a little sea magic. The most famous seashell necklace was Ursula's golden one, of course. Her power almost defeated Triton's, but thankfully it was destroyed." The mermaid shuddered at the memory.

Mal nodded and took Ben's hand and pulled him away to catch up with the rest of the group. She didn't want any mention of villain history to mar their day, and Ursula's evil actions still cast a shadow on the Seaside community, in the same way that Audrey's grandmother had snapped upon seeing Mal, the daughter of Sleeping Beauty's famous nemesis, attending school in Auradon.

They found their friends in front of a booth selling scoops of Seaside's famous clam-shaped fried ice cream. Arabella had taken on the role of unofficial tour guide, and was telling Evie, Jay, and Carlos which flavors tasted the best and which ones to avoid.

"Plankton is a good choice; it tastes like pistachio,"

Arabella said, tapping the glass and pointing to the nearest tub.

"Sounds good, I'll take it," said Carlos.

Jay leaned over the counter. "What about that one?" he asked, motioning to a dark-colored flavor.

"Oh, that's anemone. It tastes like chocolate."

"Nice, I'll go with that one," said Jay, nodding to the merman working the counter. He watched as the merman scooped up a hefty roll, placed it between two crusty pieces of bread, closed it up like a clam and tossed the entire thing into the fryer, then stuck it on a Popsicle stick and handed it to Jay to eat.

Jay bit into it and smiled in satisfaction. "Wow, how does it keep from melting?" he asked.

"Magic," said Evie. "Kidding. The bread keeps the heat away from the ice cream like a shield. It's simple chemistry."

"Which one do you want, Mal?" asked Ben. "My treat. Let me guess. Purple starfish!"

"Good guess!" she said, squeezing his hand.

"One purple starfish coming right up," he said with a smile. "I'll have the same," Ben told the clerk.

Mal took a bite. It tasted like lavender and honey. Delicious. Evie and Arabella chose the whitecaps flavor, which Evie reported tasted just like vanilla except with a little more sea salt. The group left the ice-cream counter and slowly made their way through the crowded aisles of booths, admiring colorful pieces of sea glass and scrimshaw sculptures.

"Hey, what about this?" said Carlos, picking up a T-shirt that proudly proclaimed, "I Went to the Seaside Festival and All I Got Was This T-shirt."

"Perfect," said Evie. "Especially since it's in black and white."

"Of course!" said Carlos, tossing the shirt over his shoulder.

The next booth sold CDs of blue-whale songs, and Carlos picked up a set of headphones to listen. "I wonder why they haven't switched to offering it on a digital streaming service yet," he said.

"Oh, you know blue whales, they're a little old-fashioned and set in their ways," explained Arabella. "But you guys should head back to the aquatic auditorium to catch the start of the one-million-meter butterfly. The mermen swim so fast you can't even see their fins! They're just blurs in the water!"

"You're not joining us?" asked Evie.

"I have to say hi to my family. My grandfather's hosting a reception under the sea," said Arabella. "I'll catch you at the free-fin race."

The mer-games were just as thrilling as Arabella promised, and Mal cheered with the rest of the crowd as the merfolk showcased their speed and strength in a number of races and competitions. Evie decided she liked the synchronized fin dancing best, while the boys enjoyed the underwater boxing matches, which were projected on a screen since the other audience members couldn't actually go underwater to watch them like the mermaids did. The free-fin race was just about to start when a flash of lightning forked the sky and a crash of thunder rolled, booming so loud it echoed all over the open-air stadium.

Ben looked up with a frown at the suddenly dark skies. "Huh, that's weird. All the weathermen predicted sunny skies for today," he said.

"But isn't it always sunny in Auradon?" asked Mal.

"Not today," said Carlos, as seemingly out of nowhere, an angry storm gathered above their heads, turning the clouds black and sending sheets of rain all over the color-ful tents and booths and drenching everyone seated in the auditorium. The merfolk dove into the sea while everyone else rushed to the exits.

"Let's get out of here," said Ben, removing his jacket to use as an umbrella over their heads. "Follow me to the limo!"

They ran out toward the parking lot, where cars and carriages were gridlocked as everyone tried to get out of the rain and leave the festival at the same time. The five of them piled into the royal limousine, drenched and shaking from the cold, wet droplets soaking the leather seats.

"Where did that storm come from?" said Evie, her bangs

plastered to her forehead. "There were blue skies just a second ago."

"Where's Arabella?" asked Carlos.

"She texted me earlier. She said she was going to stay a little longer at her grandfather's party and not to wait," said Evie, checking her phone again. "She's with her family."

"We need to get home before it gets any worse," said Ben.

Mal agreed. "Yeah, let's go." Outside, rain lashed the windows and a furious wind howled, rocking the car. The exuberant celebration of underwater life had ended, literally, with a wash.

"So much for the festival," said Jay.

"It's too bad," said Evie. "They worked so hard to make it special."

Mal kept silent. In her pocket, the Dragon's Egg throbbed and turned warmer. Was it connected to what was happening outside? She hoped not, but the freak rainstorm made up her mind. As soon as they got back to school, it was time to say goodbye to the evil talismans, once and for all.

chapter

2

A Sudden Wild Magic

It stormed for the entire trip from Seaside to Auradon City, but when they finally arrived at Auradon Prep that afternoon, the skies were as blue as ever. As the limousine pulled up to the school, Mal turned to her friends. "You guys, I think it's time we dealt with the talismans."

"I was hoping you would say that," said Evie, making a face as she removed the golden apple—now a tarnished bronze—from her purse. "I've been carrying this for a few days and it gives me the creeps."

"I don't know, it's kind of fun having them around; it reminds me of where we came from," said Jay, unearthing a twisted wooden stick with a cobra head from his pack. Its snake eyes were leering and baleful, even in stasis.

"Well, unlike you, I don't want to be reminded of the Isle of the Lost all the time," said Evie. "Do you have yours, Carlos?"

Carlos nodded but looked nervous. "Yes, unfortunately. I wanted to leave it in my room because I don't like carrying it around, but it felt like too much of a risk." He showed them the plastic ring he had in his pocket.

"I have mine," said Mal, removing the glowing Dragon's Egg from hers.

"Great, I'll let Fairy Godmother know we're on our way," said Ben.

"Right," said Mal, taking a deep breath as they all got out of the car.

There was only one way to deal with the talismans; only one power in Auradon that was stronger than evil, tougher than wretchedness, and more tenacious than malevolence. A force that could turn a kitchen girl into a princess, tiny mice into a team of king's horses, and a simple pumpkin into a wondrous carriage. The most powerful magical artifact in all of Auradon: Fairy Godmother's wand, wielded by the most powerful magic-user in the land: Fairy Godmother.

They entered campus and headed to the main building, where they trooped into the office of the headmistress. The cozy, comfortable place was decorated in shades of princess pink and periwinkle blue, and even the curtains sparkled with starlight. There were cozy plump couches to sit on and many framed photographs of Fairy Godmother and her daughter, Jane.

"Welcome back! How was the Seaside Festival?" asked Fairy Godmother, getting up from behind her desk and smiling at all five of them. "Did you give King Triton my regards?"

"I did," said Ben. "The festival was wonderful as usual, except for this strange storm at the end."

"I saw on the news," said Fairy Godmother. "What a shame." She nodded to the four villain kids holding out their talismans. "So there they are, huh? I've been expecting them."

"Sorry, we got distracted by school," said Mal.

"Absolutely understandable. It's not as though I were looking forward to this task either," said Fairy Godmother, shaking her head. "Oh dear, what a collection. You are all heroes for surviving their temptations." She shuddered at the sight of the pulsing Dragon's Egg. "They will have to be destroyed, of course."

"The sooner the better, Fairy G," said Ben. "It's best for the kingdom."

"I suppose we have no choice," she agreed. "These dangerous objects cannot fall into their true owners' hands, but destroying them could unleash a sudden wild magic—a powerful and uncontrollable blast."

"A necessary blast," he soothed.

"But sometimes the consequences of using such great magic remain unknown until much later." Fairy Godmother sighed.

"Can we do it soon?" said Carlos, grimacing.

"What's your hurry?" said Jay with a grin as he twirled the cobra staff like a baton.

Evie shook her head decisively, her dark blue hair bobbing over her shoulders. "I'll be glad to be rid of mine. I feel like if I close my eyes I can still see all those awful things that Magic Mirror showed me."

Mal scrunched her nose. She didn't want to admit it, but the reason she had been procrastinating its destruction was because she found it strangely comforting to hold the Dragon's Egg. She understood that it was evil, and why it had to be destroyed—but it was meant for her. It was part of her heritage, part of her mother. And so a part of Mal—a very small part, but there nonetheless—would lament its demise.

"Right, no time like the present," said Fairy Godmother, and they followed her out of the office. She led the group toward the Museum of Cultural History, where her wand was once again kept safe and secure, floating in a crystal case.

"Bibbidi bobbidi boo," said Fairy Godmother, and the case disappeared, allowing her to pluck her wand from the air. "Hold them out, please," she ordered.

Mal, Evie, Carlos, and Jay stood in a semicircle, talismans balanced on their palms. Fairy Godmother scratched her head with her wand for a minute, thinking hard. Then with a flourish she waved the wand above the talismans, showering glittery sparks all over the room.

> *"Salagadoola mechicka boola,*
> *Send this apple back to its tree!*
> *Salagadoola mechicka boola,*
> *Destroy this ring of envy!*
> *Salagadoola means mechicka booleroo,*
> *Stop this cobra from hissing forever!*
> *And the thingabob that does the job*
> *Says this Dragon's Egg will hatch never!"*

Fairy Godmother pointed her wand, shooting an arc of light over the talismans that wrapped around them like a mini tornado, and as the power grew, the room became hot with magic.

The light turned into a ball of flame that reached into the ceiling, and with a piercing, high-pitched noise that shattered every window in the museum and caused everyone in the room to put their fingers in their ears, the light burst through the roof and out into the sky, and the four talismans erupted in a huge explosion of sparkles that showered everyone in shiny, powdery dust.

When the smoke cleared, Fairy Godmother waved her wand toward the ceiling and fixed the hole, and then turned to the windows.

"Whoa," said Mal, rubbing dust from her eyes and coughing.

"Do you like my hair this way?" Evie joked, and Mal realized they now all had frizzed hair that stood on end. Carlos's was practically a Mohawk.

"Everyone all right?" asked Ben, wiping the glittery soot from his shoulders.

"Yeah, I guess," said Jay, who was on the floor looking for his beanie, which had been knocked off his head by the force of the spell.

"I think we're okay for the most part," said Carlos, coughing and holding his sides.

"Mal, you look a bit woozy," said Ben, concerned.

In truth, she felt as if she'd just been punched in the stomach by the loss of the Dragon's Egg, but she gave him a brave smile. "Evie?" she asked, turning to her friend, who was a bit pale.

Evie nodded, but her smile was strained. The loss of their talismans had affected them all.

"Well, let's hope the only damage was to the ceiling and windows," said Fairy Godmother with an anxious smile. The pink bow around her neck was slightly singed. "Like I said, you never know what happens when this kind of wild magic is unleashed."

"I'll ask the council and all the kingdoms to keep an eye out for anything out of the ordinary. Thank you, Fairy Godmother," said Ben.

Mal straightened her jacket, a troubled look on her face. "But what about the dome remote control that got left on the Isle of the Lost? If the goblins on the island ever get it to work, Cruella De Vil, Evil Queen, Jafar, and all their minions can still get off the Isle."

"Hmm, that is a puzzle," said Fairy Godmother.

But Carlos was bouncing on the balls of his feet, his face lit up with excitement. "I thought of that, and I was worried too, until I remembered something." He held up a small black electronic device and fiddled with the buttons.

"What did you remember?" asked Jay, curious, and looking over Carlos's shoulder.

"Codes can be reprogrammed. Even if they get the remote to work, they won't have the new code to open the dome," said Carlos with a grin. "I already took care of it."

"Just like magic!" said Evie.

"Nope, just like science," said Carlos, with a nod to Fairy Godmother, who strongly advocated that the residents of Auradon learn to live without depending on magic.

"So we're safe now, right?" asked Evie hesitantly.

"Safe and sound," said Fairy Godmother. "Except for the exams coming up."

There was a communal groan as Ben and the villain kids remembered. You could save the kingdom, but you still had to pass Magical History.

chapter

2 1/4

A Sudden Wild Magic, Indeed

The burst of magic that shot through the entire kingdom of Auradon was so strong and so unexpected that no one on the Isle of the Lost even noticed when the invisible barrier disappeared for a moment. (Well, it *was* invisible, of course.) It frizzed out of existence, and for that glorious minute, everyone who was trapped on that island could have escaped from it. Except no one knew, and so no one escaped, because no one noticed.

Except for the fish down below, who found it odd that something that had previously been on the other side of the barrier had now floated over to the Isle side. The side where the villains lived, the side where evil ruled, the side where, if anyone had any idea that this certain something was now within grasp, the entire ocean would soon fill with scoundrels of all sorts trying to get their hands on it.

And that is exactly what came to pass. . . .

Because someone or something . . . *did* notice. . . .

Someone with a big mouth.

chapter
3

A Fishy Story

"A pint of pond scum, two brine balls, a bucket of chum, and a side of rot," the old pirate said, perusing the menu with his one good eye.

"Rot: Dry or wet?" asked Uma, all business, pencil poised above her notepad.

The pirate thought about it. "Wet."

"Terrible choice," Uma growled. "Order in!" she called, placing the ticket on the revolving machine by the kitchen window.

"Order up!" the cook growled back. She was a surly woman in a white chef's hat and red apron who slammed every order on the table with a bang so that half its contents spilled on the floor. The shop's menu was posted on wooden planks over the counter, listing items such as sea slime, spleen, and grit, as well as their specials, shell smell and fish guts.

Uma picked up the tray, tucked the pencil behind her ear, and saw to the other patrons in the drafty, perpetually damp tavern that always smelled like fried fish. Long wooden tables and benches were filled with pirates and louts. A seashell throne stood in the far corner; it had been made for her mother and was now Uma's favorite place to sit. She'd been working at the restaurant for as long as she could remember, watching her mother broil offal and roll out the dogfish dumplings. But while Ursula's name was on the sign at the door, she was hardly ever there anymore. These days Uma's mother spent most of her time at home watching Auradon soap operas on their rusty television and mourning her glorious past when she lived in King Triton's palace. Ursula had been exiled from Atlantica before being exiled again to the Isle of the Lost, a double banishment that she swore to avenge.

Uma was glad to have the place to herself. If Ursula were around, she would only be raging and complaining about why she had been saddled with such an ungrateful and useless daughter. Ursula never ceased to remind Uma how often she'd lost to Mal. When she'd learned Mal had been chosen to go to Auradon, Ursula flipped her tentacles. Uma never heard the end of it.

Uma cleared a few tables and kicked out some pirates for dueling, pointing to the sign on the wall that said NO DUELING. A few minutes later, she returned to the old pirate's table laden with his meal. "Pint of scum, brine balls, boiled chum, and a side of wet rot," she said, banging it all down on the table.

The old guy sniffed at the plate of brine. "This smells a week old," he said suspiciously.

"It is a week old," said Uma, her arms crossed.

"Excellent!" he said, and dug into his rather disgusting-looking meal. Uma had no idea how people could eat at Ursula's. *You'll take it how I make it* was the house slogan, and so far, no one had the courage to complain. Many on the Isle remembered the power the sea witch used to wield.

Uma continued to "serve"—more like yelling and dumping food in front of a few more patrons—a couple of hungry Huns sharing a plate of moray soufflé and a few rowdy Stabbington cousins fighting over the tastiest pieces of splat. When Uma returned to the pirate's table, his plates were empty and the old sea rat was rubbing his belly in appreciation. "Hey, you heard the news?" he asked, seeming to be in a talkative mood.

"What news?"

"Goblins have some hot info," he said, leaning in to whisper.

Uma rolled her eyes. "Goblins are terrible gossips." She kept clearing the table, stacking everything on her tray.

"Yeah, that may be, but they sure have an interesting tale to spin this time," said the pirate. "Rumor going around the docks is that it's got something to do with the merfolk."

"Oh yeah?" Uma couldn't help being intrigued. For all intents and purposes, she herself had merfolk blood. *Queens of the seas,* Ursula would lament. *We would be queens of the seas if not for that awful Triton and that terrible Beast.*

The pirate raised his eyebrow and grinned. "You know that storm we had yesterday? The big one that almost tore down the mast of the *Jolly Roger?*" Uma nodded. "Something weird about that storm; it came out of nowhere, ripped through all of Auradon and the Isle of the Lost. Goblins say a couple of eels over by Seaside saw a fool mermaid playing around with King Triton's trident and accidentally created that downpour—and lost the trident in the process."

She pursed her lips. "Lost trident, huh? I call fish tale," she said, putting away the tray of dirty dishes and crossing her arms. "Everyone knows all the magical artifacts in the kingdom are kept in the Museum of Cultural History. Triton doesn't even use his trident anymore. The golden age of magic is over in Auradon."

The old pirate scratched his silver beard. "Doesn't he take it out for every mer-festival?"

"He does," Uma had to agree. She'd seen the sea king on TV, holding up his trident at the opening ceremony.

"And when was the festival?"

"Yesterday," Uma allowed, recalling the incessant

coverage on the Auradon News Network. They'd even pulled that stupid crab out of retirement so he could sing that song one more time.

"Ended with that big storm," said the pirate.

"But if Triton's lost his trident, why doesn't he just call it back up?" she asked. "Can't he do that?"

The pirate smiled a crafty smile. "He sure can, except he doesn't know it's gone yet. None of the merfolk do. Whoever took the trident isn't owning up to it. No one knows how, but some goblins swear they saw it right by the edge of the barrier, and that it somehow floated over on our side. Which means it's currently adrift in the waters around the Isle of the Lost!"

"But how did it get here? Through the barrier? Nothing can pass through that thing, not even underwater," said Uma skeptically.

"Mystery, isn't it? But the goblins swear it's true. Something must have happened over in Auradon," said the pirate. "Now everyone's looking for that thing. Including me." He grinned. "What would Triton give to have it back, right?"

Uma's eyes narrowed, her thoughts racing. If the goblins were right, and the pirate wasn't lying, then a golden opportunity had fallen into the Isle of the Lost. Triton's trident was one of the most powerful magical objects in all of Auradon. Even if its magic wouldn't work on the Isle, it was still valuable.

A thing like that could change her life. If Uma could

get her hands on it, it would mean she wouldn't have to stay here at the fish shop, slinging the house bilge and pouring drafts of slime. Her hand automatically reached for the locket she wore around her neck. Inside was a tiny piece of junk that her mother had given her as a child. "It's all I have left," Ursula had said at the time. Uma never understood why a sliver of metal mattered so much, but she liked holding it when she was anxious.

An idea had formed in her wicked little mind. Her mother had taught her about the power of negotiation, or as she'd described it, talking someone out of their greatest treasures and giving nothing of value in return.

If Uma found Triton's trident, she could use it to negotiate her way out of this island once and for all. She could offer it up to King Ben in exchange for release from exile.

How would she get her hands on it, though? It was underneath the waters around the Isle of the Lost, which meant she would have to find a ship and a crew, and a way to retrieve it before anyone else found it.

But for now, there were stacks of dishes to wash (or at least rinse), plenty of grime to collect for tomorrow's brew, and lots of crabgrass to sauté for Crab Surprise. (The surprise was that there was no crab in it!) Until she figured out a way to get to that trident, she was stuck on land, with nothing to show for her life but a bucketful of pond scum.

chapter

4

The Girls from the Isle

The next morning, Evie woke up early to get ready for class. Back at Dragon Hall, professors expected their students to be late, and chided them if they were early. *The early bird catches the worm, but the tardy bird* steals *the worm*, was one of the school's oft-repeated pieces of wisdom. But Evie was in Auradon now, and getting up with the sun suited her. She'd worried her hair wouldn't recover from the shock of frizzing when the talismans were destroyed, but it was her usual lush, cerulean mane after she'd washed and blow-dried that morning. Evie pulled on her favorite finger-less gloves, stepped into her stacked-heel boots, and looked over with a fond smile to where Mal was still sleeping, her purple locks peeking out from under a pillow that she always placed on her face to keep the light out.

With a satisfied sigh, Evie smoothed the duvet on her bed to make sure it was perfect, admiring her sewing machine sparkling in the sun by her desk. She straightened her garment rack full of dresses for clients and pinned up a picture of Queen Belle's signature yellow frock to her inspirational pin board filled with photos of various princesses. Mal's side was a little messier in comparison, with sketchbooks and paints thrown around the rug and a little graffiti over the headboard to make it feel like home.

Evie left the room, taking care not to wake Mal, and grabbed breakfast and a cup of chirpy-as-your-smile coffee from the happy workers at the cafeteria—a decided improvement from the black-as-your-soul lattes served up by the goblins back on the Isle. After, she headed to her first class: Life Skills without Magic. She saved Mal a seat next to hers, which remained empty even as the bell rang and class began.

Good Fairy Merryweather was writing some numbers on the board when all of a sudden the clock on the wall flew back to the top of the hour and an unexpected wind blew through the room, sending everyone else back to where they had been fifteen minutes ago. Evie blinked, and the seat next to her was suddenly occupied. Mal sat there with an innocent look on her face, just as the bell rang, right on time for class.

"Mal," Evie said in a scolding tone.

"What?" Mal replied, even as she was holding a well-worn brown tome etched with a golden dragon on its cover.

"You're using your spell book again, aren't you?" she said accusingly.

"Hmmm, it appears that time-turning spell needs some work," Mal muttered, as Evie peered over Mal's shoulder to watch her write *Those with villain blood appear to be immune* in the page's margin.

Evie shook her head. "Time turning?"

Mal looked sheepish. "It only turns back time to the top of the hour, and only if it's been less then fifteen minutes. More than that and nothing happens, as I discovered the other day, when I was late and got detention," she said in an aggrieved tone.

Detention at Auradon Prep wasn't meant to be a real punishment like it was at Dragon Hall—but Evie knew that to Mal an hour of cake baking with Professor Merryweather was as bad as it got.

"Relying on magic can be a dangerous habit," Evie whispered, as Merryweather started lecturing on points that would be covered in the exams next week. "That's what Fairy Godmother says. If you solve all your problems with magic, we never learn how to solve problems on our own."

"But isn't that what magic is for?" Mal whispered back. "To solve problems? Isn't that what Fairy Godmother did, when she sent Cinderella to the ball in a fabulous dress? Or when Beast turned from a monster to a handsome prince? Or when Aladdin got on a magic carpet and showed Jasmine a whole new world? Or even yesterday, when Fairy Godmother destroyed the talismans?"

"No," said Evie, sounding even more convinced than ever. "I don't want to lecture, but that's not what magic is for. Magic is an expression of the unlimited capacity of mystery and wonder in the world. Cinderella's goodness brought the Fairy Godmother to her, and Belle's love for Beast transformed him, and while Aladdin was able to charm Jasmine with the magic carpet, remember when Genie turned him into Prince Ali and he almost lost it all? A dependence on magic can be a weakness. It's not for skipping a tardy mark. The talismans were a special case."

Mal chewed her pencil. "Okay."

Evie put a hand on Mal's arm. "I'm just trying to help."

"I will try next time, Evie, I promise. Tomorrow," said Mal, putting a hand on top of Evie's and squeezing it.

Evie nodded, satisfied. They turned their attention back to class. The Life Skills exam would test them on the proper way to balance a checkbook without resorting to arithmancy, or even worse, a calculator. Merryweather stood at the chalkboard in front of a column of complicated numbers. "Now pay attention, because this is important. A balanced ledger means the number on this side equals the number over here. The test will have a list of credits and debits for you to balance."

"What's a checkbook?" Evie whispered.

"A book filled with checkmarks?" joked Mal. On the island, all transactions were done in trade or through the goblins, who kept meticulous records.

They giggled softly together, and Evie was glad that they were both equally clueless about normal Auradon life.

"We've got to get better at this," said Evie determinedly, copying down the numbers from the chalkboard.

"Maybe it's too late for us. We're the girls from the Isle, after all," said Mal thoughtfully.

"But our future is in Auradon," said Evie.

"True. But I still know where we came from," said Mal.

"I do too," said Evie, as she went through the calculations and balanced her ledgers perfectly. "But now I'm more interested in where we're going." She flashed her friend a reassuring smile, which Mal returned.

"Yeah, you're right, you're more Isle Light," said Mal.

"Isle Light?" teased Evie. "Is that some kind of soda?"

Mal laughed and they both finished their study sheets. At the end of class, they walked out together, running into Evie's boyfriend, Doug, in the hallway.

"There are my favorite girls," he said, slinging an arm around both of them.

Mal raised an eyebrow.

"Ahem, I mean, my favorite girl," he said, gingerly removing his arm from Mal's shoulder and squeezing the one around Evie.

"She's just teasing," said Evie with a fond smile at Doug, leaning into his embrace.

"Am I?" said Mal archly.

"Hey, be nice to Doug," said Evie.

"I am," said Mal, acting offended. "When am I not nice to Doug?" She turned to him. "You did really well during the band performance at the tourney game the other day," she said sweetly. "I think Evie particularly enjoyed your jazz solo."

"Thanks, Mal," he said, beaming.

"Anyway, I should go," said Mal, hugging Evie goodbye. "I forgot I have to meet Ben at the royal library opening. Do I look okay?"

Mal was wearing a purple T-shirt and leather pants, not exactly grand-opening, meet-the-public material, but Evie knew she didn't have time to change. "You look beautiful!" she said, and that was the truth. Mal always looked great, even when she was wearing a preppie punk dress for a royal event.

Mal smiled hopefully. "Wish me luck!"

"Luck! You'll do great!" said Evie.

"Luck!" called Doug. They watched as Mal sauntered away.

Doug looked fondly at Evie. "Speaking of luck. How did I ever get so lucky?"

"What do you mean?" she asked.

"Um, band geek on the short side wins hand of Isle princess?" he said lightly.

"All that matters to me is that you're a prince at heart," said Evie. "You really think I'm a princess?"

"Your mother is Evil Queen, right? That makes you a princess."

"Thanks, Doug," said Evie, blushing. "I guess I thought it didn't count in Auradon. No one ever remembers I actually am a princess." She realized she never got invited to any of the royal functions—she was overlooked for the princess tea the other day, and while Evie would never say a word, she did have bona fide royal roots, as Doug pointed out.

"I remember," said Doug. "How can I forget? You're the fairest in the land."

Evie felt a spark all the way down to her toes. "Okay, stop, now you're making me blush," she said. "And late for my next class."

They said goodbye, and Evie hurried to Advanced Goodness, when she heard someone call her name. She turned around to see Arabella fiddling nervously with the edge of her shirt. "Evie, I need help," she said.

With her messy, uncombed hair and red-rimmed eyes, she was a far cry from the put-together Arabella from yesterday, who had been proudly showing them around Seaside.

"Sure! What's up? Do you need another dress made?" asked Evie. But something in the look on the little mermaid's face told her that this particular problem wouldn't be so easily fixed by a dress with a lace bodice and a leather skirt.

chapter
5

Royal Engagements

"Ah, there you are, Sire," said Lumiere, handing Ben a pair of gem-encrusted scissors.

Ben thanked his servant and excused himself from the ambassadors from the Bayou de Orleans, who'd come all the way from Grimmsville to attend today's event.

"Is Mal here?" he asked, making his way to the front of the podium, where a polite crowd of students and librarians had gathered, along with the royal press corps, ready as usual with cameras flashing and television microphones.

"No, Sire, not yet," said Lumiere.

"Let's give her a minute," he said.

"I think we need to start," said Lumiere. They were already running half an hour late, and the guests were getting restless. "I will bring her up when she arrives."

Ben agreed, taking the scissors and standing in front of the big yellow ribbon that was draped behind him in front of an open doorway. He looked out at the expectant faces gathered around, as well as the television cameras and phones that were held up to record his every word.

"It's a real treat to be here today at the opening of the royal wing of the Auradon Library. As you know, my mother is an avid reader and believes books are passports to a deeper knowledge and understanding of the world," he said, giving a speech he'd performed so often he could recite it in his sleep. (There were many royal library wings in Auradon.)

After the speech, Ben shook hands and made polite conversation with the dignitaries, keeping one eye on the entrance, looking for Mal. They hadn't seen each other since Fairy Godmother destroyed the talismans yesterday, and he wanted to make sure she was all right. She'd seemed a little green around the edges after the spell had cleared. He hadn't had any time to text her that day yet; his royal schedule was so packed between classes and royal duties that he hadn't even had a second to himself, so he'd been looking forward to seeing her at the library at least.

Ben wondered what was keeping her as he walked over to the buffet table, perusing the hot hors d'oeuvres, pie, and pudding flambé. All his favorite foods. He picked up a cup of the flaming pudding and spooned a bite. Ben had learned to take every opportunity to eat at these royal events; he'd been to a reception in Agrabah once where he had passed on food offered at the pre-ceremony, not knowing about the traditional six hours of speechifying that would follow. By the time they finally served dinner at midnight, he thought he'd pass out.

Ben was also looking forward to seeing Mal so he could ask her to be his lady and have her official debut at Cotillion, an Auradon tradition that was coming up in a month or so. He was a little nervous about it, but it wasn't like he was asking her to publicly declare her love for him in front of the entire kingdom. Except, well, he was. Maybe that meant he should make his Cotillion proposal a little more special? But before he could think more on it, he was pulled aside by some older ladies from the Aurora Priory who wanted to have a word.

"How is your dear mother?" asked a duchess, who counted herself among Belle's closest friends and was something of an aunt to Ben.

"She's very well, thank you," said Ben. "I think she's looking forward to coming home; she said she's been a bit seasick on the last leg of their cruise."

"I'm so glad," said a countess, who was another of his mother's close friends. "The kingdom has missed them."

"I've missed them," said Ben, feeling a bit homesick for his parents. He was proud they trusted him enough to leave the entire kingdom in his hands, but once in a while, he did miss having his family around.

"Oh, sweetheart!" chorused the ladies, who immediately took to comforting him like their own child.

Ben was assuring them he was quite all right when he felt another tap on his shoulder and turned to see Lonnie. "Ben, can I have a word?" she asked.

"Sure," he said, relieved to have an excuse to bid good-bye to the well-meaning mother hens. "What's wrong?"

"I just got a message from the Imperial Palace. There's some trouble in Northern Wei's Stone City, near the Great Wall: a border dispute with Agrabah."

Ben frowned. "That doesn't sound good."

"It's not. The Emperor doesn't want to insult the Sultan, and they're both asking if you can help them come to an agreement," said Lonnie. "The villagers on both sides will listen to you as King of Auradon, without anyone from the Imperial Palace or the Sultan's family losing face."

"Sounds like a plan," said Ben.

"Will you come now?" she pleaded. "The Emperor is worried the situation might escalate. So far everyone is being polite, but he thinks it'll be more than that if people don't calm down soon."

"Yes, of course." He wiped his mouth with a napkin and

set down the pudding, following Lonnie out the door just as Mal rushed in with that determined look in her eye that he loved.

"Ben!" she cried when she spotted him. She looked as if she'd just been running.

"Mal!" he said, happy to finally see her.

They hugged.

"Am I that late? Are you leaving already?" she said, stricken. "I'm so sorry! I thought it was at the main library, not the school library. I went to the wrong place!"

"No, it's okay. Don't worry. The event isn't over, but I do have to go," he said, motioning to Lonnie.

"Oh, hi, Lonnie," said Mal.

"Hi, Mal," said Lonnie, fidgeting anxiously with the sword on her hip.

"What's wrong?" Mal asked.

"Trouble between Agrabah and Northern Wei. I've got to broker a peace deal between them and the empire," said Ben.

"We have to leave immediately," said Lonnie.

"How long will you be gone?" asked Mal, just as her phone burst into a devilish laugh. *MUAHAHAHAHA. MUAHAHAHAHA.*

"Interesting choice for a text alert," teased Ben.

"Yeah, I'm not so into the standard chirping bird," said Mal, looking down at her phone. "Huh, Evie just emergency-texted me. I should go too."

"Let me know if you need anything," said Ben. "I don't know when we'll get back yet, so keep in touch."

"I will, don't worry," Mal promised, looking up at him with her sparkling emerald eyes. "And good luck."

They hugged again, and Ben kissed her forehead. "By the way, remind me, I have to ask you something when I get back."

"Okay. Why so mysterious?" asked Mal. "Just ask me now."

"I want to make it special," said Ben with a smile.

"Ben, we should really go," said Lonnie anxiously.

"Go," said Mal. "You're needed."

Ben nodded and gave her a final squeeze, then ran off to follow Lonnie out the door to make the necessary arrangements with Lumiere.

chapter

6

Hooked on a Feeling

"Coming through, coming through," Harry Hook called, flying down the banister to his next class at Serpent Prep, the tails of his red waistcoat flapping as aspiring henchmen and teenage toughs scurried out of the way, lest they be unfortunate enough to have a chance encounter with Harry and his hook.

The Serpent Preparatory School for the Education of Miscreants, as it was appropriately named, had many terrible students—a host of evil, wicked, scheming, rotten little villains, who were just like their parents. But in all of Serpent Prep, there was only one Harry Hook.

Harry laughed his maniacal laugh and waved his hook merrily, slashing at the air, as a little first-year tripped trying to get out of his way. Harry himself landed on his feet, and with a flourish, tipped his black tricorn hat and bowed to a group of young witches who tittered at the sight of him. "*Hiiiii*, Harry," they chorused in a melodic singsong.

"Ladies." He winked, his smirk making them swoon. Dark-haired, with a wicked gleam in his dark eyes that were roguishly lined with guyliner, Harry had all the swagger and swashbuckling charm of a real devil-may-care buccaneer. He was the only boy in the Hook family—right between his older sister, sassy and mean-spirited Harriet, and his younger sister, CJ (short for Calista Jane—the baby—who was always off having grand adventures of her own). Harry prided himself on being wild and unpredictable, off-kilter and a little mad, his one disappointment being that he hadn't come by his hook naturally—he had to suffer the injustice of having to *carry* a hook in either hand.

He'd tried to entice Tick-Tock to take a bite of him once, hanging off the dock and dipping a hand in the water, but the lazy crocodile just opened one eye and went back to sleep.

Entering the classroom, Harry slid into his seat next to Uma, who was already in her usual place in the back of the room. "Well, *helloooo*," he drawled.

"Arr," she grunted, looking irritated.

Harry wondered what was wrong. Uma was his oldest

friend on the Isle. She'd sort of decided to order him around when they were kids, and he sort of fell into the habit of following her orders. They had a lot in common: cruel intentions, awesome pirate outfits, and well-muscled arms. Plus, they were always up for mischief and adventure.

This was their favorite class, Accelerated Piracy: Hostage Taking and Threatening. But today's lesson was all about different pirate flags, which could honestly put any swash-buckler to sleep.

Uma could usually be counted on to cause a little trouble and a little excitement, and Harry wished she would shake herself out of this dark mood she was in. There were gob-lins to torment, rigging to swing around in, and victims to rough up out there. He couldn't do it alone.

"Want to go see if we can find some first-years to walk the plank?" he asked. "Or raid Jafar's Junk Shop?"

Uma shook her head. "Not today. Today I need a ship."

"A ship! What do you need a ship for?" he asked.

"We're pirates, Harry. What kind of pirates don't have a pirate ship?" she said.

Uma had a point. A pirate's life on the Isle of the Lost was a bit limited. There were no rich galleons loaded with gold to attack, no merchant ships to hold hostage, no ports to raid. If they had a ship, their pirating would still be restricted, true, but the invisible dome that kept the island apart from the mainland fell a little beyond the immedi-ate shores, which meant a ship could still sail from one end of the island to the other, maybe even to the Isle of the Doomed, the haunted island that nobody visited.

"Think of all the awful things we could do if we had a set of sails," said Uma. "Especially if we ever got out of the Isle of the Lost. We'd have the freedom to do bad deeds everywhere!"

That did sound promising, thought Harry. Freedom to rampage and adventure—explore the world and steal its finest treasures. "All right, we need a ship, but where would we get—?" he said, just as he remembered a flyer he'd ripped from the school bulletin board earlier that morning. He unfurled it from his pocket, studying it carefully. "Look at this," he said, nudging Uma.

It was a ship, or more accurately, a drawing of a ship. A pirate ship with black sails, flying the Jolly Roger and everything. A real beauty.

"*The Lost Revenge*," read Uma.

"Good name for a pirate ship," said Harry approvingly.

They read the rest of the text together.

PIRATE RACE
FIRST MAN TO REACH DEAD MAN'S
COVE FROM THE GOBLIN WHARF WINS
THE *LOST REVENGE* FROM THE ONE
AND ONLY CAPTAIN HOOK
IF IT FLOATS, USE IT AS A BOAT!
TO ENTER: BRING TREASURE!

"This is it!" said Uma, eyes alight. "I'm winning that ship!"

"You?!" said Harry, almost choking on the word and falling off his chair. "This is a ship from my dad's fleet! That ship should be mine!" Of course his father couldn't just *give* him the ship, could he? Instead Captain Hook was using it to amass more bounty. "And you'll need a crew to sail that thing!"

"I'll get a crew!" howled Uma, slamming her palm on his desk. "Isle of the Lost? This is more like Isle of the Lemmings! Everyone here is just looking for someone to follow, someone to look up to, someone to fear! Now that Maleficent's a lizard, there's no one in charge! Why not me? I'll have a crew faster than you can say *octopus*!"

"But you don't even know how to sail!" Harry protested.

"And you do?" sneered Uma.

"Of course I do!" yelled Harry. "I'm a pirate! You're just a sea witch!"

"I don't care! That ship is mine!" said Uma.

"No, it's mine!" said Harry, as they each took hold of the paper's edge and pulled it toward him- or herself.

Uma let go of the flyer, taking Harry by surprise, and he lost hold of his hook, which rolled to the floor. Quick as Lucifer, Uma pounced on it and held it high. "It's mine!" she said triumphantly.

"Give it back," growled Harry, seething.

"Oh, I'll give it back . . . *if.*" Uma said, a dangerous smile creeping on her face. She looked so much like her mother at the moment that it gave Harry chills.

"If?" he squeaked.

"If you or I win this pirate race, I'll give you your hook back," said Uma.

"And if we don't?"

"If neither of us win, your hook is gone forever. I'll throw it in the ocean. And if I win, you work for me as first mate. I can't sail a ship, but you can," said Uma.

Harry considered the offer. "So if you win or I win, I get my hook back," he said. "And if you win I have to work for you."

"Uh-huh," said Uma with a salty smile. "Like I said, you'll be the first mate on my crew."

"If *you* win," reminded Harry. "If I win, you'll be *my* first mate."

"You're not going to win," said Uma smugly, crossing her arms. "I always beat you."

"I might," said Harry. "I'm fast."

"Slippery, more like."

"Slippery is still fast," Harry said with a winning smile.

"So it's a deal?" said Uma, keeping Harry's hook behind her back while she held out her hand.

"Deal," said Harry, shaking it. "Now tell me why you really need that ship." He knew Uma well enough to know she wasn't telling him the whole story. They'd been pirating all their rotten lives, and she'd never been interested in a pirate ship until today.

Uma leaned in and told him an unbelievable story about a missing golden trident and how they could bargain their way off the island with it.

Harry listened attentively without yawning or interrupting. But at the end of her story he did have one question. "Okay, say we do get that ship. How are we going to find that thing in the water?"

She waved her hand dismissively like Ursula did whenever she had to cast away any doubts in her victims' minds. "I'll figure it out later."

"You really think we'll get off this island?"

"If we play our cards right," said Uma. "Negotiation is my specialty."

Harry scratched his cheek with a fingernail, thinking it over. He wasn't sure exactly what he'd agreed to, but however it turned out, he'd probably get his hook back, and he already missed it. "All right, let's go put some rafts together then," said Harry, studying the flyer again. "The race is this afternoon."

chapter

7

Fairy Goddaughter Casts a Spell

Amerman in a gold scale-patterned uniform came flying at him, sending the ball toward the goal, but Carlos blocked it quickly, throwing it back into the melee. Jay caught the ball with his paddle and ran down the field, jumping on shields, dodging every defenseman and cannonball shot in his path, until he successfully sent the ball whizzing into the Seaside goal. *Yes!*

But the Seaside team quickly recovered. Carlos was still celebrating Jay's score when another merman came barreling toward him, almost certain to score. The ball shot toward the very edge of the goal, and right when it seemed all was lost, Carlos flew up and slammed it away from the net, just as the whistle blew to end the game.

Auradon Fighting Knights 3, Seaside Mermen 2.

It was the final game of the season, and they had just won the championship against the number one seed. Carlos cheered, jumping up in the air and waving his paddle. He pointed at Jay. "You!"

"You!" cheered Jay, removing his helmet and rushing across the field to thump Carlos in the chest. They laughed and joined their team in a group hug, a sweaty huddle of excitement and adrenaline.

Then, like the good sports they'd learned to be, they joined their teammates in consoling their opponents, who were congratulating them. "Good game, good game," Carlos said, high-fiving the defeated mermen as they streamed by the Auradon Fighting Knights.

"Yo! Bomb Goalie!" yelled Herky, a rather large teammate.

"Huh? What did you call me?" asked Carlos.

"Bomb Goalie! You're the goalie, and you're the bomb!"

"Ha! Nice one, thanks," said Carlos, pounding his teammate's outstretched fist. Herky enthusiastically tapped him back, sending Carlos flying right into the path of the Auradon mascot.

"Oof!" said a distinctly feminine voice from inside the Fighting Knight costume.

Jane! Carlos thought, rushing to see if she was all right.

"I'm so sorry!" he said, helping her stand back up. Jane removed her costume helmet and shook out her hair.

"Are you okay?" asked Carlos.

"I'm fine," Jane said with a laugh. "Risks of being the mascot." Her dark hair was plastered to her cheeks and neck and she was all sweaty, but Carlos thought she looked sweet.

"Okay, good." Carlos smiled. When she turned the other way, he surreptitiously smoothed down his shock of white hair. He was wearing it combed to the side these days, hoping it made him look older, more serious, and less like a computer geek.

They fell in step together off the field, Jane carrying the helmet under her arm. "Good game," she said. "Poor mermen. They haven't been having the best week."

"Did you get caught in the rain too?" asked Carlos.

"Yeah, I went with Lonnie. We got drenched," said Jane. "It's my favorite of the Auradon celebrations too."

They passed Audrey and the cheerleaders, who were squealing and holding their pom-poms while congratulating the team. Jane twirled a lock of her hair around her finger and glanced wistfully at them. "I was thinking of trying out for cheer," she said. "But that seems silly, right?"

"Why would that be silly?" asked Carlos. "You should try out if you want to."

"But I'm just the mascot," said Jane. "Mascots aren't cheerleader material."

"That's not true. Look at me, I never thought I'd make the tourney team," he told her, swinging his paddle absently.

"Really?" asked Jane. "I thought you and Jay were recruited the minute you got here."

"Jay was," said Carlos. "I was more of an accidental addition. Coach saw me running away from Dude and put me on the team. I used to be scared of dogs when I got here."

Jane giggled. "That's funny."

"See, if I can do it, you can." He smiled.

"But you're, like, brave and all," she said. "You guys stood up to Maleficent. You can do anything."

Carlos tried not to laugh at her assessment. But he had to set the record straight. "No way, I'm not brave. I was scared the entire time. Ask Jay. Or Mal. Or Evie."

Jane was surprised. "Really?"

"Yeah, I'm scared of a lot of things. I'm also scared of heights. And my mom." He shuddered.

"Aw, come on, *everyone's* scared of your mom."

"You got that right." He turned to Jane and smiled. "But cheerleaders are definitely not scary. Come on, what do cheerleaders do? I'll help you practice. Aren't tryouts for the new season next week?"

Jane nodded. "Yeah. I was thinking of maybe auditioning."

Carlos bounced across the field. "Come on, let's practice flips. I've seen you do them in the mascot costume!"

Jane laughed and stepped out of the rest of the costume,

leaving the outfit in a pile on the grass. She was wearing a T-shirt and shorts. "Okay! Let's do it!"

She did a bunch of cartwheels and backflips, and Carlos taught her how to do a one-handed cartwheel that he'd picked up from R.O.A.R. training. She taught him the Auradon cheer, and the routine that went with it, and by the end, they flopped together on the grass, red-faced and out of breath. "That was fun," said Jane.

"You're really good," said Carlos, and he couldn't stop smiling.

"You think so?" she asked shyly.

"So you'll try out?"

"Yeah. Why not." Jane laughed again. She stood up and brushed her knees, her eyes twinkling like stars from her mother's wand. "Me, a cheerleader . . . I mean, stranger things have happened, right?"

"Like villain kids going to school in Auradon?" said Carlos with a smile.

"I guess so," said Jane. "Did you ever think you guys would end up here?"

He shook his head. "Honestly, it's the last thing we expected. It was a total surprise, and we didn't even want to go." He recalled that day so vividly, how their parents had schemed and pressured them into going to Auradon as part of their evil plan.

Jane didn't expect to hear that. "You didn't?"

"No, I mean, we were raised to believe bad is good, and

all we knew was the Isle of the Lost. But our parents were determined to send us here so they could have their revenge."

"Thank goodness you guys didn't do it," said Jane.

"Yeah. It's weird. I never thought I'd be over on this side of the barrier, but it feels really natural now," he said, thinking of all the good things in his life now that he lived in Auradon. His dog, Dude, for one, and his solid gang of friends for another. *Even Jane,* he thought. If he'd never moved to Auradon, he wouldn't have met her.

"What do you want to do when you get out of here? Auradon Prep, I mean," she asked, as they left the field and walked onto campus.

"What do I want to do when I grow up?" Carlos thought about it. "I don't know. Something with computers, maybe? What about you?"

"I always thought I'd be like my mom," said Jane.

"Headmistress?"

"No, I meant like someone who grants people's wishes. But now that magic is discouraged, I guess I have to go back to the drawing board," said Jane. "Which is totally fine. Although, I was sort of looking forward to suddenly popping up when people are crying and changing everything so that they get their heart's desire."

"You like helping people," said Carlos.

"I guess I do," said Jane. She smiled and blushed, as if she'd revealed too much of herself. "Come on, race you back to the dorms. One, two . . ."

But before she even said *three*, Jane was already running, holding her mascot costume in her arms.

Carlos yelped and ran to catch up with her, following the sound of her laughter all the way to the buildings.

Jane had a sweet, lovely laugh, and hours later Carlos discovered he was still thinking about it.

chapter

8

The Little Mer-thief

After saying goodbye to Ben, Mal burst out the library doors and crossed campus, weaving her way through a crowd of students rushing out of their classes, and headed to study hall. Evie deployed the emergency-text option sparingly, so Mal knew it was serious. When she finally arrived back at their room, she found Evie sitting on the bed with Arabella, who was sniffling and wiping her eyes.

"Mal! Thank goblins you're here," said Evie.

Thank goblins? Things must really be serious if Evie was slipping back into Isle-speak. Mal took a seat across from Arabella and tried to look comforting.

"Tell Mal what you told me," Evie said to her friend.

Mal thought that maybe Arabella, who was new to Auradon Prep, had some kind of first-year problem. The villain kids all had questions when they'd first arrived too: Was it okay to eat as much food as you could from the refectory? (Jay) Could you take as many classes as you could fit into your schedule—or even take two classes at the same time, if you worked really fast? (Carlos, of course.) Evie had wanted to know if they had to wear uniforms (they didn't), while Mal's only question was where she could acquire purple spray paint (the art studio). Although it had to be more serious than that, since Evie'd texted SOS.

"I have a big problem." Arabella gulped and wiped her eyes. She was shaking. *Hmmm. Definitely not the usual freshman drama,* thought Mal.

Evie soothed. "Big problems are Mal's specialty."

"Okay," said Arabella. She took a deep breath. "Remember when I went to my grandfather's reception at the Seaside Festival yesterday?"

Mal nodded.

"So, um, I did something stupid at the party. I took something that wasn't mine," said Arabella, still sniffling. "When he wasn't looking, I swiped my grandfather's trident. I just wanted to see if I had enough power in me to use it, like my cousins. I just wanted to prove that I'm one of the king's heirs too, that I could raise the waves like he did. I figured I'd return it right after."

"Okay, so you took his trident . . ." Mal tapped her chin with her fingers; she could tell where this story was going already. The girl had gotten into some kind of mischief, obviously, but nothing too hard to untangle or fix.

"But . . ." said Evie, prompting.

"But it didn't work out that way," said Arabella, miserable. "I didn't just call up some waves. The trident was so powerful that I called up that huge storm. I lost hold of it, and it flew up into the sky—and when it fell, I couldn't find it. It washed away somewhere!"

"So it's gone?" asked Mal, shocked. *That* she hadn't foreseen, although she was relieved to discover that the Dragon's Egg hadn't been the reason behind the storm after all. Even though the talisman was gone forever, she was glad it hadn't caused any more destruction as the result of her delay in taking it to Fairy Godmother.

"It's gone." Arabella nodded.

"Does King Triton know?" Mal asked. She could only imagine the sea king's rage when he found out. Mal knew all about what happened when powerful beings were bereft of their magical instruments.

Arabella shook her head determinedly. "No. I didn't tell him. I didn't tell anyone. I was too scared."

Mal nodded. "I can imagine." The sea king's anger could make the very seas boil with rage.

"But isn't he going to find out soon? I mean, it is his trident."

"I told him I put it back in the case, which he's going to return to the museum tomorrow."

"Okay."

"So I only have until tomorrow night to get it back," said Arabella. "Before Grandfather finds out it's missing."

"And you haven't told anybody?"

Arabella shook her head. "My mom would kill me . . . and so would all my aunts, of course. I saw it shoot into the air, but no one seemed to notice because of the storm."

"They probably thought it was just lightning," said Evie.

"So what exactly do you need us to do?" asked Mal.

"Help me find it?" Arabella said weakly.

"We have to help her," said Evie.

Mal considered it. Arabella should probably tell her family what happened as soon as possible, but Mal understood wanting to take care of something on your own, or with the help of your friends. Speaking of friends in need, Ben was on his way to Northern Wei, and Mal didn't want to bother him while he was on such an important trip. But she could still rely on the rest of the gang.

"Evie, let's get the boys," said Mal.

Arabella's face lit up with hope. "So you guys will help?"

Mal nodded. "Of course we'll help. Any friend of Evie's is a friend of ours."

chapter

9

Race to the Bottom

own by Jailor's Pier the docks were filled with sloops and schooners, brigs and clippers, vessels of all kinds and shapes, some driven by sail, others by paddle. They crammed the bay, anchor lines stretching in every direction, the boats rocking back and forth as the wind caught this one or that one. A galley with fifty paddles rowed past Uma, the men chanting in time, the oars beating the water. Seagulls filled the air with their shrieks, adding to the cacophony of chants and mixing with the hawkers' cries from their stalls. Uma crouched on a makeshift raft she'd fashioned from one of the shop's old tables, a broom handle, and a bedsheet. It was seaworthy enough to sail on the bay for a small race, but would not be able to handle more than that. A great cutter sailed past her, and its wake nearly sent her tumbling overboard. Next to her, Harry was bobbing up and down in a bathtub, using a shower curtain for a sail. The wake half-filled his tub, and immediately he had to bail furiously to keep the thing from sinking. Even empty, the tub barely floated. It hung at water level, and each time it tipped, a bit of water ran into it. All in all, he'd done more bailing than sailing, Uma noticed with wicked glee. It was all he could do to keep afloat.

"Let's go over there," she told Harry, leading them through the assortment of ships. They passed a few goblins on an old junk, one of those ancient boats from Northern Wei, sporting a red sail like the fin of some exotic fish.

"Check that out," said Uma, as the junk sailed out of their path to reveal a pair of witches sitting in great buckets rowing with giant spoons.

"Where do you suppose you get a spoon that size?" asked Harry. "And what's it for?"

"Well, it's for eating little boys," Uma said, coughing up her best impression of a witch's cackle. "I think your head would fit nicely on that spoon."

"I see your point. Let's steer clear," said Harry.

"Already ahead of you," she replied, sailing the other way. Neither of them wanted to get any closer to the witches or goblins.

"Looks like everyone's after the prize," said Uma, and

she didn't mean just the pirate ship. The water was full of goblins clad in snorkel gear and thugs flailing around in old fins and rusty scuba apparatuses—all of them looking for the trident, combing every bit of the ocean floor.

"So many," said Uma, her heart sinking a bit in her chest. News of King Triton's trident had gone out, it seemed, and half the island was looking for the golden spear. Uma watched them nervously. Some had maps and others had formed groups. They were drawing grids across the bay and moving zone by zone, covering every inch. They were all as eager to find it as she was, and that worried Uma. *The whole island's gone mad for the trident,* she thought, *and while I'm trying to win a boat, they're already combing the sea.*

Next to her, Harry whistled at a goblin swimming by the junk. "Ahoy! What sort of *junk* are you looking to find?" he asked with a grin.

Harry must have been hoping the goblin would take him up on the joke, but he received an honest reply. "A trident! Haven't you heard?" said the green little fellow.

"That golden thing? I heard the mermen saw it on the other side of the Isle!" Harry said, then winked at Uma. He whispered, "Thought I'd throw them off the scent!"

"Wonderful," she replied, rolling her eyes. "There are hundreds looking for the trident, maybe more, and you've thrown *one* off course."

"It's a start," said Harry, shrugging.

Over by the edge of the harbor, Captain Hook had

finally made his appearance. He sauntered down one of the larger docks, the planks creaking beneath his weight, the wind at his back. He wore his characteristic red jacket and an enormous red hat with an even larger white plume dangling over the brim, swaying this way and that as he walked.

"Dad really knows how to make an entrance," said Harry.

Captain Hook stopped at the end of the dock and stepped onto a soapbox so everyone could see him. All around Harry and Uma, the competition readied itself. Henchmen wrestled with sails, ropes were flung aside or unwrapped from the docks. A great buzz of excitement and preparation built, and Uma stood a little taller in her raft. Hers was one of the smallest boats in the race, but she was confident in her victory. That ship was hers, and so was that trident.

"How are we even going to get out of the harbor?" Harry replied. "This place is so choked with boats that it'll be an hour before we sail past any of them."

"Mmm," said Uma.

Suddenly all oars were in the air and everyone's eyes darted toward the dock. Captain Hook had raised his hooked hand high into the air to indicate that the race was about to begin.

Uma gritted her teeth. She was ready. Captain Hook lowered his hand as Smee fired the starting pistol. The race was on!

A fury of sails and splashing oars overwhelmed the bay.

Sailors were yelling, goblins were giggling, witches were gaggling. It was a terrible ruckus, and the water churned, once more filling Harry's tub and threatening to drag him down if he didn't bail fast enough. "We'll never be able to sail faster than those ships on these things," Harry shouted.

"Oh, you just figured this out?" Uma said.

"And you knew that?"

"Yeah, and that's why I'm going to beat you," Uma said as she coiled a rope around her forearm. She'd fixed a noose at the end and she checked it now to make sure it would work.

Then she threw the rope high into the air. It arched over a diver, past a rowboat full of pirates, and landed soundly on a cleat attached to a small motorboat. She gave it a little tug to cinch the knot around the cleat, but there was no need. The boat's engine roared to life, and immediately the rope tightened, jerking her little craft forward. If she hadn't moored the rope to the deck of her raft, it would have been yanked from her hands. Even now it threatened to tear her craft apart. The boards moaned and creaked, but the raft held. Soon she was skipping across the waves, bounding up and down like a magic carpet tethered to a rocket.

Before she knew it, Uma was out of the bay and on the open sea. She'd chosen the fastest of the lot to hitch on to, and now they were in the lead. There was just one problem: since she was tethered to the goblins and her rope was fairly long, the *goblins* would likely win the race.

But only if they make it to the finish line, she thought.

Behind her, Harry was paddling furiously, still trying to make his way out of the boat-swamped harbor. He smashed right into one of the great galleys. Then he had to wait as more and more ships passed in front of him. By the time Uma caught sight of him again, half the bay was empty. Harry's shower curtain caught the wind, but it was too late. He was already taking up the rear. *Ha!*

But Uma didn't celebrate long. Harry's bathtub crashed into the nearest sailing ship, and he quickly abandoned it, jumping onto the catamaran. Since the ships were so crowded together, he was able to hopscotch from ship to ship all the way to the front.

Uma watched Harry's progress with narrowed eyes until she remembered she had her own problems. There was a tug on the cord and she swung the sail around just in time to catch sight of a pair of goblins gnawing furiously at the rope she'd attached to their speedboat. Once they finished, she was done, but all that gnawing seemed to be going awfully slowly and the knot was cinched too tightly for them to pull it off the cleat.

And that was when she saw the screwdriver.

She'd forgotten that goblins were clever folk. While one gnawed at the rope, the other started undoing the screws that secured the cleat. They were both in a race to cut her loose, and sooner rather than later one of them would win.

But Uma was not quite ready to lose her chance. She

pulled on the rope, yanking on it so hard that it knocked one goblin straight into the water. Uma smiled at the little green fellow as she sped past him. She yanked again, this time harder, pulling her raft closer to the goblin craft. She noticed that when she gave it a good pull, the goblins' boat jerked wildly to one side. So she pulled again as the remaining goblin worked furiously at the screws.

The two were locked in their own race now.

He'd loosened two or three of the screws, and the cleat was hanging halfway off the back of the boat. A few more screws and Uma would be set adrift in the water while the goblin claimed the prize.

Fearless as ever, Uma gave the rope another strong tug, coiling it as much as she could. When it was as tight as she could make it, she let it go, and the rope whipped wildly back into the air, snapping the goblin in the face and sending him tumbling into the water. She cackled as she passed him, just as she realized there was no one left on the motorboat.

The goblins had tied the steering wheel in place and jammed the throttle into gear while they tended to her rope. This was probably why the boat had veered to and fro when she pulled at it. There was no one to correct the boat's course. It was hers for the taking.

If she could reach it.

The cleat rattled, and one of the screws flew off. It tumbled through the air and landed with a plunk as it struck the water. Only one screw still held the cleat in place, and it was already halfway out of its socket.

She tugged cautiously on the rope. If she pulled too hard she might yank that last screw loose, but if she waited too long the screw would come loose. Either way, the boat would be gone. And the motorboat was not the only fast ship on the water. All this tugging and swerving had slowed its progress, and she saw now that two or three of the larger sailing ships had caught up to the goblin boat. Even the galley was closing in, its oars beating the water, the oarsmen chanting.

"Yoo-hoo!" Harry called with a broad grin from the top of the sailing ship barreling toward the lead.

Uma could never be his first mate!

She needed to hurry.

One tug. A second.

She pulled and pulled, and that cleat held. It whipped back and forth, pivoting about that last screw, but it was still attached. Fortunately, the force of all the pulling made the screw bend, so it had stopped twisting itself free. But now it looked as though it might break in two.

She gave another tug. One more.

She was closer to the boat. She could try to jump the gap, but it was still too wide. So she gave the line another pull, gently dragging herself toward the stern of the out-of-control motorboat.

The cleat bent. The last screw flew loose.

Uma tugged one last time, pulling herself just a little closer, and just as the whole thing fell apart she leaped through the air, arms outstretched, reaching for the stern of the boat.

She caught it! She was flattened against the back, but she hung on, and with her other arm she reached up and pulled herself aboard.

She did it!

She was at the helm of the fastest boat in the race, except she was no longer winning the race. All that fussing around had allowed three, no, four ships to sail ahead of the goblin boat, including Harry's, which was now in the lead.

Uma hurried to the helm, tore free the ropes holding the wheel in place, and jammed the throttle into gear.

chapter

10

The Jet Set

The journey to Stone City, a small village on the eastern border of the Great Wall, was past the vast forests of Eden and the Lone Keep, so Ben decided the fastest way to get there was on the royal jet. "We leave for the airport in five," he told Lonnie, who was already more cheerful now that she'd secured Ben's commitment to fixing the issue plaguing the Imperial Palace.

Ben ran to change out of his formal clothing for travel gear, trading his sash and epaulets for a royal hoodie and jeans. He wished he'd had more time with Mal, but such was the life of a king—he was constantly needed in so many places at once. He envied his parents for the length of time they'd had for courtship. Sure, Beast was hiding in exile and Belle was basically imprisoned, but they'd had all the time in the world to fall in love, right?

He would make it up to Mal, he decided, by making his Cotillion proposal extra-special for sure. He just needed a little help. *But that's what friends are for,* he thought, as he texted Jane the details of his idea.

Lumiere, who had followed Ben out of the library reception and helped get him ready for the trip, doted anxiously on the young king. "But, Sire, are you certain this is absolutely necessary?" he asked. "Why not send an envoy? Or at least bring me along."

"Not necessary," said Ben, zipping up his hoodie as they made their way out of the royal residence to the front, where the limousine was waiting. "I'll be fine. I don't want to travel heavy, and with the jet, I'll be back before dinner, if not earlier." Lumiere would be too concerned with protocol, and settling a border dispute was bound to get hairy. But Ben would be lying if he didn't admit to a small case of nerves.

Lonnie was already out front. "Thanks for doing this, Ben," she said.

"At least summon the cavalry?" Lumiere said worriedly. "They can travel on the royal speed train."

Ben shook his head, ushering Lonnie inside the car first. "If we arrive with a show of force, the villagers might not believe we're acting in their best interests. I'd like to resolve this as peacefully as I can, and if they see it's just me and Lonnie, they'll know I'm there to listen and not force them to do anything they don't want to do."

Lumiere looked as if he wanted to keep protesting, but he decided against it. His shoulders slumped, as if lights had been extinguished on a candelabra. "As you wish, Sire."

"Don't worry, Lonnie's with me," said Ben with a smile. "She'll keep me safe."

Lonnie motioned to the sword strapped on her back. "Nothing will happen."

Chip rushed out with a bag of snacks. "In case you get hungry, Sire," he said. "Mom packed you some sandwiches."

Ben thanked them both, and the driver bowed and closed Ben's door.

"The village elder is meeting us first, then you have a meeting with the representative from Agrabah," Lonnie told him.

Ben nodded to the driver, and the limousine left campus. A few students looked on, confused as to why the king was leaving in the middle of the school day.

The royal jet zoomed above Auradon City, flying over Charmington and Faraway Cove. "What gorgeous country-side," said Lonnie, admiring the rolling green fields dotted with golden haystacks and flocks of sheep that looked like white specks. "Do you ever think about how lucky we are to be in Auradon?"

"All the time," Ben said.

They were making good time but had to refuel, so they stopped in Notre-Dame before lunch, almost halfway to their destination. While the pilots took care of the plane, Ben and Lonnie walked over to a little square and stopped at a charming place for hot chocolates to drink with their sandwiches.

The café owners were beside themselves to discover they were waiting on royalty, and insisted the king take the best table in the house, one with a view of the church. "Please, sit, and enjoy the ringing of the bells," the waiter urged.

Ben thanked them profusely and remarked that Quasimodo's bell-ringing was indeed the best in the land. When the noonday chimes ended, they resumed their conversation.

"My family really appreciates you doing this," said Lonnie. "My mom says she wishes she could have sent us her cricket for good luck."

"Tell her thanks," said Ben, taking a sip from his cup. "I've asked a bunch of councillors to meet us on their side of the Great Wall. The Grand Vizier agreed to meet with me. It's important that they feel their voices are heard as well, since you are traveling with me."

"Good idea," said Lonnie. "I hope they listen to you. It would be a shame if things escalated."

"I hope so too, but it's more important that I listen to them," said Ben, thinking of the various issues he'd worked on since taking the throne. Most notably, he had handled the sidekicks' complaints and approved the cost of Camelot reparations after an out-of-control Madame Mim had plagued them earlier in the month.

"Is that what being king is all about?" asked Lonnie. "Listening?"

"Pretty much. How about you?" he asked. "Everything going okay?" He'd known Lonnie since they were kids, and they were almost like siblings. He remembered when Lonnie got her first sword at the age of five, and how she'd tried to stab Chip when he pulled her pigtails. Lonnie was there when Ben made his first balcony appearance; instead of waving to the crowd, he'd hidden his face in his mother's shoulder. She'd teased him about it mercilessly.

"Yeah," she said with a long sigh and fiddled with the sword at her waist.

"That doesn't sound like everything's okay," he said, concerned.

"You know how you wish you could change things, but there's nothing you can do about it?" she asked.

"Sometimes," said Ben. "But there's always something you can do about it."

Lonnie looked longingly at her sword once more. "Maybe."

"What's this all about?" he asked.

She shook her head. "You wouldn't understand."

"Try me."

"Has anyone ever told you that you can't do something just because of who you are?" asked Lonnie, as the waiter came by to offer them heaping platters of croissants and baskets of delicate pastries.

Ben considered it as he picked up a lemon tart and took a bite, smiling his thanks to the waiter. "Lots of times, actually."

"Really?" Lonnie didn't sound like she believed him.

"Yeah. When you're king, you can't just think of yourself or what you want. You have to think of the people, always."

"Always?" she said skeptically. "I thought being king meant you always got your way, actually."

"Maybe a terrible king, yeah—but not if you want to be a good one. Like, sometimes, I just really want to tell someone off, you know? Or lose my temper? Or just say what I mean? But I can never do that, because I'm the king. If I did, it would be a big deal—a yawn or an offhand comment suddenly becomes a matter of state. What I do matters more because of who I am, and so I can't ever really be myself. I have to be the king, always."

"I never thought of it that way," said Lonnie, putting down a half-eaten éclair.

"Still, I've found a way to balance being me and being king. I'm the king of Auradon, but I do it my own way," said Ben, thinking of how he had invited the villain kids to Auradon, over the objections of his parents and a host of disapproving courtiers. "So whatever it is you want, don't let anyone stop you from dreaming your dreams and following through on them."

"You sound like your mom," said Lonnie with a smile.

"I try to," said Ben, asking for the check. "She's a wise woman."

chapter 11

Biceps to Spare

Some would say it was always *unhappy hour* at the Fish and Chips Shoppe, but during the early afternoon and evening, Tears of Despair and Spoilage Brew were half off, along with discount bowls of gruel and only slightly used dirty candy. A raucous crowd had gathered around a certain table, where an arm-wrestling match was under way between Gil and La Foux Doux.

Gil, just like his father and brothers, was manly, burly, and brawny with muscles to spare, and yes—every last inch of him was covered with hair. Okay, maybe not *every* last inch, but Gil was one of the finer specimens of the Isle of the Lost, with golden hair he kept under his bandanna and that signature cleft chin. He wore a faded leather doublet that showed off his arms, with two sword belts crisscrossing his chest and leather-patched jeans that were artfully distressed in the current "pirate" fashion.

Right now, Gil was doing what he loved to do: showing off his brute strength to the ladies. He slammed La Foux Doux's arm down on the table in victory, sending the stout boy to the ground.

"What do we say?" said Gil.

"Th-th-thank you!" said the young La Foux. "Thank you, Gil!"

Gil flexed so that he made two guns with his arms and pretended to kiss each one.

Two witches sitting nearby audibly swooned.

Gil swaggered over to his table, satisfied, and ordered another round of bilge. Life was good when you were the strongest man on the island. Okay, so maybe he wasn't the smartest guy on the Isle of the Lost, but it wasn't the worst way to live.

No matter, Gil had girls to impress and feats of strength to display. He finished his meal, thinking the scum chowder was not as moldy as usual, and looked around for more entertainment.

"Who wants to see me balance the table on my head again?" he asked, lifting the heavy oak table and setting it upon his noggin. But when he turned around, the room, which had been filled with noisy revelers just a moment before, was empty.

"Where'd everyone go?" he asked, irritated.

"To watch the race," huffed the cook, pointing out the window and toward the docks.

Gil let the table down with a bang and headed toward the commotion. All week there had been talk about this race. A real pirate race, with a real pirate prize. The harbor was full of onlookers, pirates cheering each other on, and bets placed on who would come in first. Gil sauntered over to the front to watch the action, pushing people out of the way.

"Who's in the lead?" he asked.

"Harry," said one.

"Uma," said another.

Gil squinted at the horizon, where an assortment of vessels, from homemade rafts made of recovered planks with sheets for sails to a little goblin motorboat, were cresting over by Evil Queen's house. They raced toward the finish line by Dead Man's Cove in Hook's Bay, gaily decorated with old shoes and cans. There was a roar from the crowd as one pulled forward ahead of the rest, a turquoise-haired sailor raising her fist in glory as she crossed the finish line in victorious fashion.

Shrimpy? wondered Gil. *Where'd she get that goblin boat?*

"Uma! Uma! Uma!" chanted the crowd, as Uma docked her boat and stepped up to the platform.

Uma made rude gestures to the crowd to indicate her pleasure. "Thank you, thank you, thank you, everyone," she said into the microphone. "And I'd like to introduce you all to Harry Hook, my first mate!"

She brought Harry up to stand next to her. "Just like I promised, here's your hook back," she said, handing it to him.

Harry, who'd looked glum and defeated just a moment ago, lit up with a huge grin. "My hook!" he said, waving it in the air.

Smee handed Uma the keys to the pirate ship that was docked right behind them, and Harry and Uma happily climbed aboard.

Gil marveled at the thought of winning a real pirate ship, kitted out with a Jolly Roger flag and everything. Too bad it wasn't a wrestling match, or he'd have entered the competition for sure.

Harry and Uma waved from the top deck of their brand-new (actually old, shabby, and holey) pirate ship.

Gil felt a pang at being down at the docks while they were up on the ship's decks. They'd all been inseparable once, he and Harry and Uma. When they were kids, he and Harry used to follow Uma around, doing her bidding. They'd been part of a gang, but over the years Gil had drifted away from them somehow.

He melted back into the crowd and went back to showing off at the fish shop, impressing the ladies and challenging anyone to a fight. But beating his enemies in arm-wrestling matches and bullying La Foux Doux only went so far.

So when someone mentioned that Shrimpy—sorry, *Uma*, he had to remember she went by Uma now, *duh*—and Harry Hook were looking for a few good mates for their pirate crew, Gil decided to meet up with his old not-quite-friends.

"Heard you're looking for muscle," he said, his white teeth gleaming, as he swaggered up to Harry and Uma a few minutes later. He pulled up his shirtsleeves. "You're in luck, as I've got some to spare."

"Yes, we are," said Harry with a grin. "Welcome to my crew."

"*My* crew," said Uma, patting Gil on the back. "Now get with the others."

Gil climbed aboard the pirate ship, excited to find it was already filled with villains like him. Pirates, ruffians, rogues, all seeking adventure, and it looked like they'd found it.

chapter

12

swordplay

After the last tourney game ended, Jay marched back with the team toward the lockers to change, but noticed that half the guys went straight into another practice, trading helmets for face masks and carrying practice swords.

"R.O.A.R. tryouts," explained Aziz, Aladdin and Jasmine's oldest son. "You coming?" he said, tapping Jay lightly on the arm with his sword.

"Yeah, come on," said Herky, lumbering toward the mats. "We're short a couple of guys. Ben had to quit since he couldn't fit it into his royal schedule."

Jay nodded, curious about this other Auradon sport that Carlos had mentioned the other day. He followed his friends into the gym, where a few guys were already suited up, wearing sleeveless blue-and-gold R.O.A.R. uniforms and face masks. There was a spirited duel going on in the middle of the mat, and Jay watched attentively, admiring their graceful swiftness. At last, one of the sword-fighters pinned down the other one.

"I yield!" said the loser.

The fighters removed their masks, revealing their identities. The two opponents shook hands cordially, and Jay was surprised to find the winner was none other than Chad Charming.

Jay chuckled his disbelief and Chad overheard. He looked over at Jay. "You think you can do better?" he sneered.

"Can't be hard," Jay said.

"Let's see it, then," said Chad. "Suit up."

Gauntlet thrown and accepted, Jay changed into a uniform, pulled on a face mask, and picked up a sword. The sword was heavier than he expected, and a tad unwieldy as well. But, whatever, it was just Chad. He could beat Chad blindfolded.

Turned out he couldn't beat Chad blindfolded.

Instead of advancing and retreating in a line as Jay had seen fencers do before, Chad unexpectedly bounded into the wall, leaped off of it, and came around behind Jay, tagging him on the back. This caused Jay to fall, and Chad whirled around to face him. The match was over before Jay could even find his opponent.

"Yield?" asked Chad, his sword underneath Jay's chin.

"I yield," Jay spat. He tossed his mask off in frustration.

Chad laughed and helped him to his feet. "I've been training since I could walk. What do you think princes do in their spare time?"

"I don't know, sit on tufted pillows?" said Jay moodily.

"Well, that too. But mostly sword practice."

Chad left the gym, whistling.

Jay tapped his sword on the floor, making one dent after another. He hadn't anticipated such a quick defeat. He hadn't anticipated any defeat at all. He'd thought he would crush the pompous prince—a few strokes and he'd be victorious. But it hadn't gone down like that at all. He'd barely had a chance to raise his weapon and the whole thing was over.

Training—isn't that what Chad had said? The guy had been training his whole life at the sport. Chad wasn't better at this, he was just more experienced. Jay tapped the sword against the floor once more. It was time for him to start accruing a bit of that experience.

R.O.A.R. was half parkour and half fencing, and the two were not easy to mix. There was a reason fencers normally moved back and forth in neat little lines. They had swords in their hands, and even if the tips were blunted they could still do real damage if they struck you. Leaping into the air and bouncing off walls wasn't exactly what a person ought to do with a sword in their hand, but Jay guessed that was the fun of it, the challenge. Jay liked challenges.

He gripped the hilt. It was a saber, which was a heavier fencing blade, not like one of those flimsy ones that arched at the lightest touch. This one had some weight to it, so if you landed on it wrong it might just slice you, but Jay guessed that was why they wore the heavy jackets. Body armor. And he knew how to do it; he'd done it all the time back on the Isle of the Lost.

But when he tried to run up the wall this time, he fell flat on his face, and just barely missed cutting himself with the sword.

That was the problem with walls. They were rather solid things, and you were generally meant to stand next to them, not on them. He was just out of practice, he decided, so he tried again. He began with a running start, jumped, and hit the wall—planning to run up its side—but when he struck the surface, he collided into it with such force that he simply sank to the floor. Actually, he crashed to the floor. Jay turned so both of his shoulders lay flat, his eyes facing the ceiling. He had to try again. He wouldn't give up so easily.

The second jump was worse than the first. He had to toss the blade aside just to keep it from ramming a hole in

stood. The third jump yielded similar results. On the fourth
he actually abandoned the jump midway through the act.
He knew what was coming. He knew he'd have to toss the
blade, and he could see exactly how his shoulder was going
to strike that floor.

He was learning, but unfortunately, he was learning
how *not* to R.O.A.R. He tossed the sword aside and ran up
the wall easily. It was the addition of the sword that was the
problem.

"You're doing it all wrong," said a voice, and Jay turned
to see Lonnie's older brother, Li'l Shang, holding up a
sword. Li'l Shang had graduated from Auradon Prep the
year before, and was an assistant coach of the team, taking a
gap year before going home to rule his kingdom and launch
his hip-hop career. "Want some help?"

Jay was about to shake his head. His pride was bruised.
And it was still hard for him to accept help when it was
offered. No one on the Isle ever helped anyone else out. But
he had to remind himself he was in Auradon now, and they
did things differently here. Plus, it had been beyond annoy-
ing to lose to Chad Charming.

"Yeah, yeah, I guess I do want help," he admitted.

"Okay, let's start now," said Li'l Shang. The gym had
already cleared.

· 101 ·

"Should we grab swords?" Jay asked.

"I don't think you're ready for those just yet."

"Ouch, that hurts."

"I'm just being honest."

"So where do we start?"

"Well, I saw how you lost your fight. Chad made a great jump. You were trying to practice that move—weren't you?"

Jay shrugged. "Yeah, I mean I used to be able to jump, you know? But not with a sword."

"Let's practice the basics first. Each time you hit the wall or the floor you want to lengthen the time of impact, slow it down so your whole body absorbs the force. And don't just kick off with your feet. Try putting a hand on the wall. It'll keep you steady and spread out the force of impact. Same goes for the landing. Move your whole body. You need to bend your back and knees; your arms too. Remember: slow down the impact, spread it out. That's how to jump."

"Okay, so slow it down. And use my whole body."

Jay took one step, two. Li'l Shang stopped him dead in his tracks. "Take a few more steps, open up your stride and give yourself a little more height so you have time to flex your body while it's still in the air."

Jay nodded, absorbing the information. He started again. He took three steps, four, five this time—big, long strides. On the last one he leaped, trying not to stay rigid, spreading his arms, spider-like, and letting two hands touch the wall at the same moment that his feet struck it. It was perfect. He was completely enamored with himself. Unfortunately he fell straight down to the floor.

"Good start," said Li'l Shang. "Better than I would have guessed for a first-timer, but never get cocky. You hit the wall right, but you need to immediately spring backward. Take the force of your own impact and turn it around into another leap. Try again."

He did. He tried twice more, and then a third time. Each was a tad less embarrassing than the previous one. He wasn't sure how many jumps it took, but after a while the landings stopped hurting. It all started to feel natural.

Li'l Shang handed Jay back his sword. Jay accepted it gladly. It was time to move on to the good stuff: swordplay.

He leveled the saber, ready for a *real* fight.

But Li'l Shang just shook his head.

"The first thing is that you're holding it wrong," he said, fixing Jay's grip.

Jay was surprised; he thought he knew how to hold a sword.

"You shouldn't hold it that tightly," Li'l Shang continued. "You need to keep your wrist loose, keep your grip light so you can move quickly. If you hold it too tightly, you're locked into a position and won't be able to dodge or parry."

Jay looked down at his fist: he'd gripped his sword so hard his knuckles were strained white. He relaxed just a little bit and found it was easier to hold once he wasn't choking it.

"The next thing you need to remember about making the R.O.A.R. team is that it's all about balance—kind of like the jumps we practiced. But now we're using swords. It's almost like a choreographed dance: you'll learn to move on every surface, and use flips and kicks along with swordfighting," said Li'l Shang. He sprinted across the gym and launched himself against the wall, running up it diagonally, until he flipped backward and landed on his feet.

"Nice," said Jay.

Li'l Shang bowed. "It's all practice." He tapped Jay's sword with his. "En garde!" he called. "It means, *on your guard*. Every duel starts with it. It's a tradition."

"En garde!" echoed Jay.

They circled each other around the mat. "You have to be nimble, and lead your opponent. If you're just reacting to their blows, you're going to lose. You have to set the tone." He attacked with a series of lunges, moving left and right, then leaping atop a chair to land at Jay's side, pressing his sword to Jay's neck.

"Um . . ." said Jay.

Li'l Shang gave him a generous smile. "Let's try that again. R.O.A.R. isn't fencing. It's not linear. We aren't simply advancing and retreating. You can move sideways, off a wall, off anything. Think of it as 3-D fencing. Your opponent can literally jump out at you from any direction, so you have to be ready to defend yourself against an attack that could come from any direction."

"How?"

"In fencing we protect ourselves from the front, but, like I said, in R.O.A.R. an attacker can approach from any angle. So you need a whole new set of moves. The side-parry, the backward block, the over-the-shoulder cut. These are R.O.A.R. moves. Let me show you."

Shang went through each one, carefully displaying the move, then helping Jay copy it. Shang had just given him a whole new set of tools, for a whole different kind of fighting. Jay was ready to R.O.A.R.!

This time, Jay was able to not only block his coach's sword but push forward so that it was his opponent who found himself stepping backward. Jay kept advancing aggressively, the sword singing through the air as if he'd been born wielding one. He even attempted to run up the wall to dodge a blow. As he fought, his confidence grew, and he flipped, cartwheeling in the air when his coach tried to slash forward. He landed just as Shang had instructed, bending his whole body, flexing every muscle, one hand touching the floor just as his feet struck it.

"Better." Li'l Shang nodded. "Much better. We've worked on your jumps and your R.O.A.R. moves, but you still aren't bringing the two together."

"But I almost beat you!"

"I was just going easy on you. This is going to take a lot more practice on your part. Keep trying to improve your jumps and don't let the sword be a detriment to your movement. You're still too afraid that you are going to poke yourself with that thing. Use the sword as if it were part of your body. Quit holding it at arm's length. Flex your sword arm when you hit the wall and when you land. And don't separate your jumps from your attacks. Some of the best fighters will strike with their blade midway through a jump, or just as they hit the ground they'll roll into a lunge instead of planting their feet."

Jay tried a few of these moves. R.O.A.R. was definitely a hybrid sport, and it took fencing to a whole new level, but he felt like he knew the basics now. Unfortunately he was still back where he'd started: he needed practice.

"You think I'll make the team?" asked Jay. He knew he was acting a little optimistic, but he'd come a long way in a short time. How much longer would it take to master R.O.A.R.?

"Sure, if you work hard enough," said Li'l Shang. "My sister's pretty good at this stuff too. You should practice with her sometime. She just left for Northern Wei, to help with an issue there, but when she gets back you should ask her."

"Lonnie?" said Jay. "I guess I shouldn't be surprised, considering who your mom is. She's on the team?"

But Li'l Shang didn't have time to answer. The gym

doors banged open, and Carlos, Evie, and Mal entered, calling Jay's name and looking distressed.

"What's up?" Jay asked, putting down his sword. "You guys look like someone just told you we had to go to back to the Isle of the Lost."

"We might have to," said Mal.

Jay raised an eyebrow and wondered what was wrong now.

chapter
13

How Many Wonders Can One Cavern Hold?

*N*ow that she had a pirate ship and a pirate crew, Uma was in the market for a new pirate hat. Her old one had gotten way too ratty, and there was a hole on the brim that she'd covered up with duct tape. She needed something that told the world she was large and in charge. She puttered about the bazaar shops down by the central market around the Bargain Castle, looking at fedoras and trilbies, boaters and turbans. She'd brought Gil with her, who was trying on a succession of ridiculous headgear.

"What do you think of this?" asked Gil, donning a

black silk top hat. "Or this?" he said, as he switched it for a feathered creation.

She ignored him, and continued to root through the racks. Maybe it wasn't the greatest idea to let Gil on their crew. He seemed to be about three screws short of a light-bulb, honestly. But then again, he seemed very enthusiastic about doing her bidding, which was never a bad thing.

"Uma! This one, right?" he asked, strutting up in a white ten-gallon cowboy hat.

"No," she said flatly, trying on a hat of her own and considering her reflection in the shop's mirror.

"How about this one?" he said, putting on a pointy velvet hat.

"No," she said again, picking through a deep selection of tricorn pirate hats that would suit any aspiring buccaneer. She tried on a couple, but nothing was quite right.

"I think I'll go with this one," said Gil, placing a brown leather hat on his head. "Looks good?"

"Not bad," she had to admit.

"I'll take this bunch," he told the sales clerk, motioning to a big pile by the counter of all the hats he'd tried on. "They're on sale. You find anything?"

She shook her head. "I'll meet you on the ship," she said.

"Yup, see you there."

Discouraged, Uma left the shop, annoyed that Gil had been able to find something while she was empty-handed.

"What's wrong, dearie, give us a smile," barked a goon by the wharf.

"What about I give *you* a smile," said Uma, removing her cutlass and placing it just under his chin. He yelped in fear and she kicked him away, growling to herself.

Just as she turned the corner, she spotted the hat she'd been looking for. Crushed brown leather with a metal-studded brim and decorated with seashells. Sassy and stylish. It would look mighty fine with her cutlass and sword. "Yo-ho-ho!" she called. The lass wearing the hat turned.

"What do you want for that hat?" asked Uma.

"This one?" the girl squeaked, pointing to the hat on her head.

"No, not that, the other one you're wearing—of course that one!" Uma snapped, her patience wearing thin.

"Okay . . ." said the girl hesitantly, removing it from her head and holding it out.

Uma studied it, admiring its craftsmanship and detail. It really was a fine pirate's hat.

"You can have it," the girl said suddenly.

"Oh? What do you want for it?" asked Uma.

"Nothing! I don't want anything from you!" she protested. "I want to keep whatever I have, my voice, my legs, my soul, my humanity! Here, take it!" She shoved the hat forcefully into Uma's outstretched hand.

"Oh! Good," Uma said, taking it happily. "Did you make this?"

"Yes," said the young pirate, looking sad to have now lost the hat. "I washed the leather five times and picked all the seashells, then I stitched the band with a grosgrain ribbon. . . ."

Uma shrugged; all her interest had waned now that the hat was hers. She wasn't the type to make conversation anyway.

"Nice hat," said Harry, when she arrived at the ship.

Uma grinned. "Nice ship," she said, watching pirates cut down planks to the right length, nailing boards, and threading the sail.

"Sweet, isn't it?" he drawled, scratching his cheek with his hook. "At least once we patch up the holes, fix the mast, and see to the anchor, we'll be set to go. I've got the crew working day and night."

Uma crossed her arms, hoping she appeared as fierce as she thought she did. It was hard work looking this awesome. "Good job," she said to Harry.

"Good job, Captain?" he said hopefully.

"As if. You work for me, remember? Do I have to keep reminding you? I'm captain, you're first mate," said Uma, pointing a finger and stabbing his chest with it.

"First *date* if you're lucky," said Harry with a wink, pulling on his collar and strutting a little.

"Shut up," said Uma with a laugh. "And see to that sail."

Harry swaggered away chuckling. Uma knew, try as she

might, she couldn't hurt his feelings. It was all part of the game of question-and-rejection they'd played forever. But a few minutes later, Harry swiveled on his boots and returned to her side, leaning in closely. "Uma, darling," he said, in his rough brogue. "I just need to ask again—how *are* we going to find that thing in the water?"

"Leave that to me," said Uma. "Just get this ship ready." She gave him a confident smile, but she was none too pleased by that pesky reminder. How *were* they going to find that trident?

The answer came later that day—at the Fish and Chips Shoppe, no less. Uma was taking a break in the kitchen with Cook, who was feeding Flotsam and Jetsam, the two electric eels who had been Ursula's sidekicks during her glory days. The eels were swimming in their tank, below an old portrait of Ursula that hung in the middle of the kitchen, as if to remind everyone whom they worked for.

"Mama was really something, wasn't she? Back then?" said Uma. Flotsam and Jetsam nodded in their aquarium, slithering over each other.

Cook, a swarthy woman with messy red hair who always wore an ill-fitting white peasant dress with a red collar, had a faraway look in her eye. "She really was," she mourned as she cleaned a fish and saved the guts for stew.

Uma wondered what it was like, living under the sea, ruling the waves. "Those days will come back," she said.

"You think so?" Cook said hopefully.

Uma nodded decisively. "I know so. I plan to make it happen. Finish what Maleficent started, get off this island, and wreak vengeance on our enemies!" She stared intently at the golden seashell around Ursula's neck.

"Hey, do you know whatever happened to Mom's necklace?"

Cook squinted at the picture. "It got destroyed; when Prince Eric defeated your mum it shattered in a thousand pieces."

"I know that. I mean what happened to it after that?" asked Uma.

"After?" Cook frowned, setting a pot to boil and adding sea slime to the broth.

"It must be gone forever," said Uma sadly.

"Hold on. I remember now," said Cook, wiping her hands on her dirty apron. "It was too dangerous to have a thing like that just lying around, even broken. The pieces were collected and confiscated. They were supposed to go to that museum in Auradon. We heard they found the last two pieces just the other month. But then the embargo happened, so they're stuck here," said Cook, cutting up more rotten potatoes for curly fries.

Uma was intrigued. "Here? On the Isle? Where?"

"Who knows? We heard that professor, Yen Sid, was the one in charge of it. If anyone has them, he does," said Cook with a shrug.

"Professor Yen Sid has the pieces to my mother's seashell necklace?"

Cook nodded.

"Well, what's it matter anyway? There's no magic on the island," Uma lamented.

Cook considered that. "True. But just because there's no magic around doesn't mean there's no power left in it."

"What kind of power could it have?" asked Uma, confused.

Cook whispered in her ear. Uma listened carefully. When she was done, Uma raised her eyebrows.

"You don't say," she said. What Cook had told her was very interesting indeed. "Are you sure that would work? If I found the necklace and put it back together?"

"Absolutely," said Cook.

"Uh-huh," said Uma. This was it; her mother's seashell necklace was the missing link. She knew exactly how to find the trident now. Ursula's necklace was the answer.

If only she could discover where Yen Sid was hiding it.

chapter

14

Nemesis

"Wow, that's one brave mermaid," said Carlos when Mal was done sharing Arabella's story with him, Evie, and Jay after they'd pulled Jay away from R.O.A.R. practice. They were sitting at a table in the refectory at Jay's insistence, since he didn't like to hear bad news on an empty stomach. "I would never even dream of touching my mom's furs, and she goes and steals King Triton's trident? That's insane."

Jay nodded, his mouth full of food. He swallowed loudly to the consternation of the girls. "I don't mean to be rude, but why is this our problem exactly?" he asked.

"Arabella's a friend, and she came to us," said Mal defensively. "She didn't know who else to ask for help."

"Uh-huh," said Jay. "Because she did something naughty, and we're from the Isle of the Lost. But the thing is, we have stuff to do in Auradon now."

Carlos slowly nodded his head. "Jay has a point. You have a packed royal schedule, Mal. You don't really have time for something like this. Why does it have to be you—*us*—who have to look for this thing? We didn't steal it. Plus, don't forget, exams are coming up."

"And what about Ben? Doesn't this fall under his responsibility?" asked Jay.

"Ben's in Northern Wei negotiating some kind of truce between the Imperial City and Agrabah," said Mal. "I don't want to bother him with this."

The boys still looked a little wary.

Mal put her hands on her hips and scowled. "Okay, this is not the team that returned to the Isle of the Lost and defeated their evil talismans! I'll tell you why it's our problem. Because when a friend's in trouble, what do we do?" she asked fiercely.

"We leave them alone?" joked Jay. He sighed. "All right, all right."

"Come on, you guys, we all know what it feels like to have done something wrong," Evie beseeched. "And to feel scared and alone afterward."

"Of course we'll help," said Carlos.

"Yeah, we were just playing, what do you call it, devil's advocate," said Jay with a smile.

"But it seems like the best thing to do is to tell Fairy Godmother so she can alert King Triton," said Carlos. "I mean, right?"

"But Arabella asked us to keep it secret," said Evie.

"We can handle this ourselves," said Mal. "Let's not bring Fairy Godmother into it." Mal didn't want to sit around waiting to have tea with the goddesses from Mount Olympus or laughing at the Sultan of Agrabah's corny jokes again, which took up a lot of her time now that she was the king's girlfriend. She itched to do something meaningful, to be useful instead of simply decorative. "Are you guys with me?" she asked.

One by one, each of them nodded.

Mal smiled, relieved. "Obviously, first things first, we need to figure out where the trident is," she said briskly. "Any ideas?"

"That's what this is for," said Evie, removing the magic mirror from her purse. She flipped it open and spoke directly into its reflection. "*Magic Mirror of seas and skies, show me where the trident lies!*"

The mirror turned cloudy and gray and nothing happened. "Is it broken again?" asked Carlos.

Evie shook her head. "It was never broken, it just didn't

work in the Catacombs." Evie gave it another good shake, and the mirror showed the trident stuck between two rocks under the sea.

"Where is that?" asked Mal, squinting at the screen. "I wish your magic mirror could talk, Evie."

"It's only the last shard of the mirror; no audio function, sorry," said Evie apologetically.

"Looks like it's somewhere near the barrier. See that shimmering line? That's the invisible dome," said Carlos, looking over Evie's shoulder.

"Which means anyone on the Isle of the Lost could grab it, if they know it's there," said Jay.

"But where exactly is it?" asked Mal, her forehead scrunching in dismay.

Carlos took a closer look at the screen. "As far as I can tell, it looks like it's right by the Isle of the Doomed. The water's murkier over there. And see those flashes of green in the water? That's goblin slime."

Mal nodded. It was the same green color that seeped out of Maleficent's fortress.

"Those goblins would do anything to get their hands on that kind of treasure. Not to mention the pirates if they knew about it," said Jay.

"Magic Mirror, is anyone else looking for the trident?" asked Evie.

This time, the mirror's surface glowed, and showed villain after villain on the Isle of the Lost searching the surrounding waters for the trident. Witches in scuba outfits, pirates diving off docks, hooligans of all kinds swarming the beaches and picking through seaweed, searching.

"Looks like everyone's looking for it. Word must have gotten out somehow that it's there," said Carlos.

"Goblins are terrible gossips," muttered Mal.

"The worst," agreed Evie.

Jay only shrugged. He had no opinion on goblins other than that they were fun to steal from.

"It's still going," said Evie, as the mirror showed an image of a crowded tavern.

"What's that?" asked Jay, leaning over for a better look.

"Don't push!" said Carlos, as they all crowded around Evie.

"It's Ursula's Fish and Chips Shoppe," said Mal, as the mirror zoomed in more closely, until they could make out the blurry silhouette of a figure in the middle of the crowd.

"Who's that?" said Evie, catching sight of thick, ropy strands.

"I can't tell yet. One of the pirates, maybe?" said Carlos. The mirror kept focusing.

"It's a girl," said Jay decisively. "Those are braids."

"That's not a girl. That's a sea witch," said Mal, tapping on the screen.

"It's Uma!" said Jay.

"Uma!" quaked Carlos.

"Uma." Evie sighed.

"Ugh. Come on. It's Shrimpy," said Mal. "It's always Shrimpy." She told Evie about her long, nasty history with Uma.

"You know Uma's mostly mad because you said she was too small to be in our gang," Jay reminded her.

"But she *was* too small to be in our gang," said Mal defensively.

"She's not *that* small," said Carlos. "There was a height requirement?"

"Mal just didn't want to share," said Jay with a grin.

Mal shrugged, but Jay was right: she hadn't wanted Uma to be part of her crowd. She'd pushed her away, even though Uma was fiercer than Ginny Gothel and much scarier than Harriet Hook. The truth was, Uma was real competition, and Mal hadn't wanted any of that back then.

Evie squinted at the picture of Uma in the magic mirror. "Why do you hate her so much?"

Mal was taken aback. "I *don't* hate her. Actually, since we've been in Auradon, I'd forgotten all about her. She's the one who's always been obsessed with me."

Carlos and Jay nodded. "Uma *loathes* Mal," said Carlos.

"I mean, I get it, you dumped a bucket of shrimp on her head. You can't be her favorite person," said Evie. "But it's also not any different from what people on the Isle do to each other every day. Couldn't she get over it?"

Mal smiled ruefully at the memory of that fateful day. "I

think it bothered her more because we were close once, best friends actually. But then she . . ."

"She laughed at you," said Carlos, who had turned away from the magic mirror and had zipped open his backpack to get a head start on his homework. "I was with my mom that day at the docks. I saw what happened. Uma laughed at you when you tripped and fell and slid down the dock."

"Yeah, I didn't like it," said Mal, eyes glazing at the memory. "So I took my revenge. Her hair never smelled the same again. In fact it smelled . . ."

"Shrimpy," Jay said with a laugh.

Evie shuddered, thinking of how terrible that would be. "Yikes."

"I wasn't the nicest person back then," said Mal, frowning at the image in the magic mirror.

"You were only doing what you were taught," said Evie supportively. "What we were all taught on the Isle." She picked up a piece of fruit from Jay's tray and took a bite, glad that it was fresh and not rotten like they were used to on the island.

"But how does she think she's going to find that trident? She doesn't have a magic mirror at her disposal, like we do," said Jay.

"Maybe everyone who's looking for it is working for her?" guessed Evie.

"No, the goblins only work for themselves," said Mal.

"The only ones who could possibly be loyal to her are the pirates."

"A bunch of thieves and thugs," said Jay.

"Harry and Gil? You used to run with them," Carlos chided. "Didn't you?"

"I sure did," admitted Jay. "That's how I know they're all a bunch of scoundrels."

"But if any of them found it, they'd definitely give it to Uma," said Mal. "They always follow orders. Especially Harry Hook."

"We don't have much time; King Triton will notice the trident's missing by tomorrow, so we need to get it back tonight," said Evie.

"And Uma's after it, so you all know what that means." Mal stood up from the table, ready to take action.

"We need to find it before she does," said Evie.

"And hurry," added Carlos.

Jay smiled. "Here we go again."

Ocean's Elevens

Just look at the world
around you,
Right here on the ocean floor.
Such wonderful things
surround you.
What more is you
lookin' for?
—Sebastian,
The Little Mermaid

chapter

15

The Sorcerer's Snare

*U*ma paced the top deck of the *Lost Revenge* confidently. With Harry and Gil at her side, she'd assembled a solid squad—a bona fide pirate ship with a bona fide crew. No matter that Gil was so dim he often forgot not to call her by that horrid nickname; Harry and his wharf rats were ready to cut up anyone who stood in their way. She surveyed the work the pirates were doing to bring the ship up to task.

They were busy provisioning the ship, bringing on food and water from Ursula's as she'd ordered, as well as a whole host of supplies. All sorts of things could go wrong at sea, and you couldn't exactly head home if you had a problem, so they needed extra lengths of rope and sail, boards that could be used to fix the hull, and all the tools and hardware to make those repairs. Plus, Harry insisted that every inch of the ship had to be checked. Every length of rope was inspected for rents or frayed edges. Rats loved to chew on ropes, and they tended to choose the most undesirable places to snack on them. If the pirates didn't check every inch of the ropes, their main sail might just sail free the moment the wind caught it, or their anchor line might snap in two just as it took hold.

The crew went over every length of sail, and they checked all the winches and pulleys as well, making certain that each was sound, replacing a few, fixing others. They checked the mast for cracks and the rudder for soundness, and made certain it worked in proper coordination with the captain's wheel. Things seemed to be coming together. But there was one particular problem that caught Uma's attention. Apparently the *Lost Revenge* had as many holes as the ship had boards. Wooden sailing ships always take on a bit of water, she knew. But the *Lost Revenge* took on water by the bucketful, and when they'd tried to push off the dock the problem had only increased, with more water rising faster, threatening to turn her sailing vessel into a gigantic bathtub.

"So what do we do?" she asked Harry, who, coincidentally, had experience sailing in a bathtub.

"Well," Harry started, clearly excited that she had decided

to consult him on the matter. "We should have her lifted out of the water, the hull scraped clean and repainted, then—"

"Stop. That's not happening. We need to do something about the state of this ship, but we don't have time to lift it or do anything major. Be serious."

"Yeah, I guess. Okay, so then maybe it's just a matter of resealing the boards. When the ship was built, the joints were all watertight, you know, fitted together closely so no water could pass through them. But ships age, and boards flex and rot and chip, and pirate ships have a way of getting rammed into or ramming into things, taking cannon shot, the usual stuff. It ruins the hulls and the boards that make them up."

"Wonderful history of sailing, thanks, but I have no interest. Get to the point, will you?" she growled.

"We caulk the joints. There's an adhesive that's fitted between the boards and then it's all slathered over with pitch."

"*Pitch?* As in singing on key?" she asked.

"*Pitch* as in tar or mastic—what we call sludge: that black sticky stuff that water can't penetrate."

"Gotcha. Get on it," she said, pushing at his chest.

"Me?" he asked, stumbling back.

She crossed her arms. "Well, you do seem to be the expert, and I recall seeing a barrel of something black and sticky down there in the hold. I reckon you'll find all the supplies you need down there, so grab a few of the crew and get working."

"Great. I'll be covered in sludge for days."

"It beats bailing water every time we sail."

"It does," said Harry as he headed down into the hold. "I'll have this ship watertight in no time."

When Harry had disappeared out of sight, she headed to the wooden bridges and trudged back to the fish shop. Her shift was up. It was time to put away her captain's hat and put on an apron.

Later that evening, Harry, Gil, and the rest of the crew filed in. There was ferocious Jonas, with his cornrows and scar on his left cheek, Desiree, tiny but vicious in a ragged peasant dress, fierce Gonzo in his red bandanna, long braid, and blue pantaloons, crazy Bonny in her torn fishnet shirt and patched dungarees, and a whole host of others—all hardened mercenaries. They took one of the long tables in front of the kitchen window. "Recap. What do we know about Yen Sid?" asked Uma, drumming her fingers on the table.

Harry dumped a pile of documents on the table, pulled out a notepad, and paged through it with his hook. "Professor at Dragon Hall, but not a villain. *Volunteered* to live on the Isle of the Lost to, quote, 'help the new generation of villain offspring.'" At this Harry snickered. "What a loser."

"What else?" said Uma impatiently.

"Let's see," said Harry, having trouble turning the pages

with his hook. Uma sometimes wished he would give up with the whole hook obsession and just use his hands, but she knew it would never happen.

"Here we go," said Harry. "Keeps to himself, amateur lepidopterist."

"Lepidop-what?" said Gil.

"Studies butterflies," explained Harry. "You know, those bugs with the pretty wings?"

"I know what a butterfly is," growled Gil.

"Really? Well, you learn something new every day," said Harry with a smirk. He continued to read the list. "What else, let's see . . . has never set foot in the Fish and Chips Shoppe, but is a regular at the Slop Shop, where he takes his tea."

"Tea?" Uma made a face.

"Yeah, it annoys the goblins to no end, because they're a coffee shop, and apparently he always insists on chai, which of course they don't have," said Harry. He kept reading. "No known acquaintances. No associates. An enigma, shall we say. . . ."

"Hold on, what's this?" said Uma, picking a paper off the top of the pile. It was marked with a golden beast-head stamp and signed by Fairy Godmother.

Harry peered over her shoulder. "Oh, those are transfer documents—for when he moved here to the Isle of the Lost from Auradon. I had one of my boys pull the file."

Uma pointed to an additional name on the paper. "Look."

Harry read the file and caught Uma's eye. They grinned at each other, matching evil smiles. "This is it. This is how we get in."

"What?" asked Gil, still oblivious and his stomach growling loudly.

Uma studied the document again. This was all coming together beautifully. She could see the outline of a plan already. Truth be told, she was a little afraid of the esteemed professor. There was a hidden strength and a fortitude to the old guy that chilled her, and the scope of his magical power was legendary. For once she was glad there was a magical barrier to protect them from such wizardry. There was no way they would ever get her mother's necklace back from the sorcerer himself; Uma knew that for a fact. Yen Sid would never let that happen. But here on paper was another way. "Professor Sid didn't move here alone," said Uma slowly.

"He brought his apprentice!" added Harry gleefully.

Uma held up the file. "The Sorcerer's Intern."

"We just need to find out who he is and where. We'll never get the professor to talk, but this is the weak link. His apprentice is sure to know where he keeps that necklace," said Harry triumphantly.

Gil studied the grainy, blurry picture. "She."

"She?" asked Uma.

Gil nodded in excitement, happy to contribute to the planning. "I know her, she helps out Professor Sid in class.

Like a teacher's assistant. Sort of quiet, shy, a little mousy even. Always sweeping. Sophie, I think her name is."

"Great! Let's see, we can threaten, bribe, or intimidate. What do you suggest?" asked Harry gleefully.

"First things first," said Uma, thinking quickly. "Gil, invite her to the Fish and Chips Shoppe tonight. Tell her we stumbled on a bit of magic and want to discuss it with her before alerting her boss."

"Discuss?" Harry asked innocently. "Is that the word for tying someone up and threatening them with my hook?"

Uma smirked. "Don't worry, Harry, you'll have your fun." By the time they were done with her, this Sorcerer's Intern would wish she'd never set foot on the Isle of the Lost.

chapter

16

Lad and Lass

il had never had any trouble asking girls to go out with him. In truth, most of them went out of their way to make themselves available. Girls were always dropping schoolbooks in front of him, or giggling uncontrollably in his presence. He was used to a certain amount of admiration from the female species. But when he approached Sophie after class that day, she was wary.

"What do you want, Gil?" she asked, setting down the books she was holding and pulling up the red sleeves on her robe. She had dark hair and a skeptical expression. "I'm not giving you the answers to next week's test, if that's what you're asking."

"Oh, too bad," said Gil, before catching himself. "Wait, no, that's not what I wanted to ask you."

"Well, what is it, then? I've got study notes to hand out and quizzes to return to the professor," said Sophie impatiently.

"Wanted to know what you're doing tonight," said Gil, throwing her his most dazzling smile. He flexed a bicep for good measure.

"Tonight? I'm refilling the professor's well. Exciting, isn't it?" said Sophie dryly. "I'll be carrying buckets of water all night."

"I've got a better idea. You, me, and the Fish and Chips Shoppe," said Gil.

"Huh? Is that like a date?" asked Sophie.

"What, you've never been on one before?" asked Gil.

"I've been on dates!" said Sophie defensively.

"Okay then!" said Gil. "I'll see you tonight!"

"No. I told you, I'm busy," said Sophie, turning away.

This was not going as planned, and Gil began to sweat. Uma would not be pleased if he couldn't get Sophie to come out tonight. "But you have to go!" he whined.

"Why?" asked Sophie.

"Because I really like you?" Gil blurted.

Sophie stared at Gil. "Really?"

Gil smiled, then slapped his forehead. "No! I mean yes. I mean, also, Uma's got something magical that she wants to show you."

"Something magical? There's nothing magical on the island."

"Well, she has something," Gil insisted.

But Sophie clapped her hands and suddenly looked delighted. "Does she have it? We've been looking for it everywhere!"

Gil had no idea what "it" was, but figured correctly that the right answer was "Yes!"

Her wan face glowed. "Great! I'll be there. But she better return it," warned Sophie. "I need it back as soon as possible!"

"Okay," said Gil, relieved it had all worked out. Now Uma wouldn't yell at him. Uma could be scary when she felt like it, which seemed to be always. "See you there!" he said enthusiastically, hoping that somehow Uma had whatever Sophie was looking for.

chapter

17

Rug Burn

"King Ben is here! King Ben is here!" The villagers of Stone City left their work and dwellings to line the road near where the royal jet had landed. Ben got out and waved to his people, who waved and cheered back. They walked together in a merry parade all the way to the center of town. After hours of sitting, it was a relief to finally arrive at the peaceful valley in the middle of Northern Wei. Like its name, all the buildings and houses in Stone City were made of rock, and the village itself had been built near a giant mushroom-shaped stone. The Great Wall loomed over the north side of the village, casting a long shadow.

They passed the city gates that led into the greatest

pavilion, and followed the cobblestoned path all the way to the front of the structure, where the town's leaders were waiting to greet them.

Elder Wong, who wasn't a gray-bearded official in a smock, but a young man who wore his dark hair in a ponytail and was wearing a natty suit, bowed upon seeing Ben. "Thanks so much for honoring us with your presence," he said.

"Charlie?" Ben asked, delighted. "You're the elder of this village?"

"Hey, man," said Charlie, slapping Ben a high five. "Yeah, went home and took on the role. Looks like you did too," he said, motioning to the golden circlet that Ben wore as his traveling crown.

Charlie had been a few years ahead of Ben at Auradon Prep, and Ben was glad to find an old friend in unfamiliar territory. Maybe this dispute could be settled easily after all.

"Hey, Lonnie," said Charlie. "How's Shang doing?"

"Still coaching R.O.A.R. and trying to get that hip-hop record out," said Lonnie, giving Charlie a hug.

"Nice," said Charlie. "Come on in, let's talk over boba."

Ben and Lonnie followed Charlie inside the stone house, which, while ancient and minimal on the outside, was outfitted with the latest gadgets inside. Ben spied a large-screen television on the wall, a roving robot sweeper on the carpet, and a high-end security system with a twelve-camera display. Charlie led them to a small room with a view of the mountains and a portion of the Great Wall.

Charlie sat cross-legged on the floor in front of a low table that had been set for them with the village's finest china and silver, and Ben and Lonnie did the same.

Instead of diving right into the business at hand, Ben and Lonnie regaled Charlie with the latest news from Auradon.

"Is it true that Audrey's dating Chad?" said Charlie, shock written all over his face. "Whoa."

"Yeah, although I hear Audrey's changed her mind about him," said Lonnie with a laugh.

"Oh no, really?" said Ben, who hadn't heard that rumor. "Poor Chad! He'll be crushed!"

They talked about the Seaside Festival, and Charlie mentioned the Imperial Palace was looking forward to hosting Ben during their Auradon celebration. "I hear they've hired acrobats from all over the kingdom," said Charlie. "Especially the ones who can do tricks with fire."

Lonnie smiled. "The fire dancers were always my favorite."

"Yeah, I can't wait," said Ben. "It's going to be amazing. Too bad Seaside got rained out."

"It happens," said Charlie.

"So what's going on here?" asked Ben, accepting a tall glass of boba from a smiling servant. He sipped the round tapioca balls through the extra-large straw.

"See up there?" asked Charlie, putting down his glass and pointing out the window. "Those dots in the sky? They're flying carpets. You think they'd be quiet, right? But they fly so fast they can create a sonic boom. So every time one of them flies over the wall to our side, everything in the village shakes. It's horrible. Babies cry, things fall off tables, and see that cluster of trees over there? They're olive trees. They're planted on the Agrabah side of the wall, and when the carpets fly over, they shake the trees."

"Uh-huh," said Ben.

"Some of the olives fall over on our side then," said Charlie. "So we use them. But our neighbors over there say that the olives are theirs, if not for the wall blocking their ability to harvest them. They want their olives back, and, well, we don't want to give them back. They're on our side of the wall, fair and square. Plus, the carpets are a nuisance—a huge headache. We're sick of it. We've asked them to ground the carpets, but they refuse."

Lonnie raised her eyebrows and looked to Ben, who scrunched his forehead and chewed a bubble of tapioca before answering. "Why do they need carpets? They never use them anywhere else in Auradon," said Ben.

"Because of the wall over here. The carpets are the only way to get over it without having to go all the way around."

"I see. And you guys eat a lot of olives?"

"Enough," said Charlie. "My villagers are doubly annoyed because the branches and leaves of the olive trees shed in the winter, and who has to clean up all the mess? We do, because they fall on our side of the wall. The Sultan's people don't offer to clean it up, do they? No, they just want to fly their carpets and eat their olives without any of the work."

Ben leaned forward. "And what are you guys doing about it?"

"So far, nothing yet. Just shouting from opposite sides of the wall. But we're prepared to do more. We've stationed archers on the wall," said Charlie defensively.

A servant placed a tray of food in front of them. There was olive bread, olive oil, and a fragrant, olive-scented roast beef. Ben reached for a hunk of bread, tearing the loaf, and bit into a piece, just as the entire room began to shake with a boom from a flying carpet. "This is delicious," he said. "And I can see why you find the carpets aggravating."

Charlie relaxed slightly. "I'm glad you understand the situation. I was a bit worried about the response from Auradon. To be honest, I wasn't expecting to see the king."

"Lonnie asked me to take charge personally," Ben explained.

"Then we have you to thank," said Charlie to Lonnie, who bowed and smiled.

"Ben will do right by us," said Lonnie. "Won't you, Ben?"

Ben wiped the crumbs from his hands with a napkin and rose from the table, grunting a little from the exertion of having to stand from the floor. He was careful not to promise anything without meeting with the other side first. If this issue was going to be resolved, he needed to figure out a fair way to appease both sides.

"Thanks much for your hospitality," he said, shaking Charlie's hand. "I'm meeting with the Agrabah delegation next, and then I'll get back to you guys."

"Great. We look forward to settling this issue once and for all," said Charlie. "We know you'll do your best."

Ben nodded. He meant to be a king for all his subjects, which meant keeping the interests of the villagers from Stone City in mind as well as the grievances of the people of Agrabah when he made his final decision. He hoped they would abide by it.

chapter

18

A Spell for Every Occasion

"We need to steal a boat from the dock," said Jay. "How else are we going to get out into the ocean?"

"Steal? No way!" said Mal, who was leery of embarking on a plan that might get them in trouble, especially while Ben was away. They'd been in Auradon for a few months now, and no one looked at them as villains anymore. They were just regular students like everybody else. She hoped they could solve this the Auradon way and not resort to tactics they'd learned on the Isle of the Lost.

"We'll just borrow one," suggested Evie. "Right?"

"But who do we know that owns a boat?" said Jay.

"Um, Ben does," said Carlos. "He has the royal fleet at his command."

"And we only need one boat," said Evie.

"Okay, let me try him," said Mal, taking out her phone. Borrowing a boat sounded like an excellent, Auradon-approved idea. Ben would surely allow them the use of one of his boats, and, as Evie pointed out, they only needed one. Mal dialed his number, but instead of ringing, the line gave her a busy signal. She typed a text instead. But it bounced back as well. "Hmmm. I can't get through. He's over at a village near the Great Wall," she said.

"Yeah, they don't have good signal in the outer provinces of Northern Wei," said Carlos. "I doubt you'll be able to get ahold of him in time."

"Like I said, we'll just steal one, and once we're done with it, we'll bring it right back," Jay insisted. "There's no other way."

Mal crossed her arms and put away her phone, frowning. "I guess not." She still didn't like the sound of it, but there didn't seem to be another alternative. *Goodness is as goodness does,* Fairy Godmother liked to say, and Mal thought that if their intentions were good, that counted for something. Right?

"There really isn't any other way for us to get out there," Evie said reluctantly.

"Not unless we turn into mermaids," said Carlos, shrugging.

"Great!" said Jay, clapping his hands together. "Let's go!"

"But we have to be really careful that we don't get caught," said Mal, as they hurried out of the cafeteria together.

Jay shook his head. "Come on, it's me! Just a few months ago I was the best thief on the Isle of the Lost. And did I ever get caught?"

They all had to admit the answer was no.

Jay almost felt nostalgic as they made their way down to Belle's Harbor that night. Getting past the guards stationed at the entrance to the royal marina was easy. They had done enough slinking and scurrying around in the shadows on the Isle of the Lost that they were experts in hugging walls, crouching, and scampering when someone was looking the other way. They ran down the gravel path toward the water, coming to a stop right at the gate before the dock.

"It's locked," said Mal, tugging on the handle.

"Not a problem," said Jay with a smile, as he held up his trusty pin. He was enjoying being able to indulge in his old bad habits once more. But as much as he twisted and turned and shook the pin inside the lock, it wouldn't open. "Huh," he said. "That's never happened before." He removed his beanie in frustration.

"Let's just climb over it," said Jay, already scampering up the iron mesh. The rest of them tried to do the same, but the gate was too tall, and the steel cut painfully into the palms of their hands. Even Jay had to quit halfway up the gate.

Carlos slid down with a yelp, and Evie almost twisted her ankle trying to get a foothold.

"This isn't going to work," said Mal, trying to stop the bleeding on her knuckles.

Jay kicked at a pebble, frustrated.

Mal looked around to make sure there was no one around. "Step aside, I'll just spell it open." She removed her mother's trusty spell book from her pack and paged to the right incantation.

"Toad's breath and vampire's tickle, open up this door a little!"

The gate swung open an inch, and Mal smiled.

"Nice work," said Jay, pushing the door open. "After you, ladies."

Evie looked concerned as she stepped through the gate. "Mal, you're really using that spell book more than you should."

"I'll stop after today, I promise," said Mal, as Jay and Carlos followed after them and ran ahead to check out the different kinds of boats.

"Which one do we want?" asked Jay, as there were sailing and motor vessels of all kinds. He rubbed his hands in glee at all there was for the taking. There were cabin cruisers, sleek sailing catamarans, fishing trawlers complete with outriggers, and even a hydroplane.

"I don't know, just something that will get us there fast," said Mal.

"How about this one?" asked Jay, whistling at the sight of the crowning glory of the royal collection, a fancy two-hundred-foot yacht complete with a helicopter pad on the top deck.

"We're not taking that," said Mal.

"Why not?" Jay asked, annoyed. He was already picturing himself in the captain's seat, and he would bet there was a sweet royal Jacuzzi up there.

"It's the royal yacht," said Mal. "It's saved for only special occasions. Ben would kill us."

"Fine," he said, sulking.

"Hey guys, how about this one?" Carlos called from farther down the dock.

They rounded the corner and found Carlos grinning from a sleek black speedboat with the royal insignia on the side. BEAST'S FURY was carved in gold on the stern.

"It looks fast," said Jay, hopping on.

"Faster than a pirate ship, hopefully," said Mal. "Uma cannot have that trident. Who knows what she'd want for it!"

"She'll want to get off the island for sure," said Evie.

"And we cannot have her rampaging around Auradon," said Mal. "Think of the trouble she'd stir up."

"Just one problem," said Jay, glancing around the dashboard of the elegant boat. "We don't have the keys to this thing."

"Again, not a problem," said Mal, consulting her spell book once more. "Hmmm, what kind of spell do you think would work? Key-making spell? Boat spell?" She flipped through the pages. "Oh! How about this one? My mom's notes said she used it all the time before she came to the Isle to turn on the microwave when it didn't work."

Mal held her hand up and pointed to the boat. *"Lizard's tongue and demon's spawn, make this blasted thing turn on!"*

The boat's engine purred to life. Jay grinned and gave her a thumbs-up.

"Just one problem," said Carlos. "None of us actually know how to drive a boat. And I'm not sure there's a spell for that."

"Hmm, maybe not," said Mal. "But let me check."

"I think that's probably enough spells for the day," said Evie delicately.

"But we'll need the spell book to get through the barrier, and then to call up the trident," Mal reminded her.

"Need what to do what?" a voice called, just as a bright light shone upon them on the shadowy dock, temporarily blinding all of them.

Mal frantically motioned to Jay to cut the engine, and the four of them froze in place, barely daring to breathe.

"Who's there?" called the increasingly familiar voice. "Show yourselves!"

Mal shielded her eyes and looked up past the light to the person holding the spark. She knew that wand.

"Oh no! It's Fairy Godmother!"

chapter

19

The Sorcerer's Secret

*U*ma had worked at the Fish and Chips Shoppe her entire life, from when she was so little she could barely see above the counter, until she was old enough to wear an apron, carry a tray, and take an order. She recognized most of their regulars, and when new customers walked in, Uma always paid attention. So when the Sorcerer's Intern entered on Gil's arm, Uma spotted her right away.

She and Harry were whispering by the counter when they arrived. Uma nodded to Gil, who waved back and signaled for Uma to come over. She shook her head. She wanted Gil to talk to Sophie for a little bit, soften her up before Uma went in for the kill.

Harry slunk away and Uma went back to work, slamming down trays and yelling at patrons who dared not to tip, pointing to the sign—TIP OR ELSE!—that hung by the exit. After an hour, Gil sidled up to the counter that Harry was leaning on and Uma was wiping with a rag. "Are you ready to talk to her yet?" he asked Uma, a desperate tone in his voice.

"Why, are you out of conversation?" Uma asked.

"Almost! We've been sitting over there forever. I did what you said. She thinks we're on a date. Keeps asking me about my hobbies and whether I enjoy long walks on the beach. I've seen a lot of pictures of her cats," he groaned. "I told her you wanted to chat now."

"Fine. Harry, stay close in case I need you." Uma squared her hat on her head and walked over to the table, to where a young woman in a red wizard's robe was seated, sipping bilge and snacking on a side of fried clams. "Hi, Sophie?"

"Hey, Uma," said Sophie. "These are great! What do you guys put on them?" she said, motioning to the plate of clams and wiping her mouth with a napkin.

"You don't want to know," said Uma frankly. "I mean . . . Cook has a fabulous recipe." She realized that buttering up the clams, so to speak, was the way to get what she wanted from this girl. "Did you guys have a nice dinner?"

"We did," said Sophie. "I've never been here before."

"Come back again," said Uma. "On Fridays we have the weekend special." The weekend special was everything that didn't sell over the week, but Uma didn't say that.

"Okay, I will," said Sophie. "I don't really get to go out too much."

"The sorcerer keeps you busy?"

"Yeah, there's always papers to grade and research on his experiments. But I have nights and weekends off. It's just a bit far from where we live."

"I see," said Uma. "I heard you're not from here, like we are."

"Yeah, I'm not. My family's from Eden, actually," said Sophie. "We live in the middle of the forest."

"Do you miss it?"

"Sometimes. It's so green back home and so . . . well . . . not green here." Sophie shrugged.

"You don't have to say," said Uma. "We know what the Isle is like." She whistled to a server. "Bring us two pints of the best swill."

"Oh wow," said Sophie.

"My pleasure," said Uma. "Gil is handsome, isn't he?"

Sophie's eyes flicked to Gil, who raised his bilge glass to her with a goofy smile. "Yeah, I guess, if you like brawny."

"Who doesn't?" said Uma.

Sophie giggled self-consciously. "Belle, I guess. Although she married Beast."

Uma decided it was time to get down to business. "Anyway, you have a second?"

Sophie nodded and put away her napkin. "Gil said you had something magical for me," she said, in a professional tone.

"He did?" Uma was confused for a moment until she remembered it had been her idea to tell Sophie that she had something for her. "Oh, right, I do."

"You really have it?" Sophie asked, her neck tensing at the question. Whatever it was that she thought Uma had, it was clear it was incredibly important to her.

Like Gil, Uma decided the best answer was a definitive "Yes. I have it."

"Oh, thank wizards!" said Sophie, smiling in relief. "I've been looking for it everywhere! Where'd you find it?"

"Around," said Uma vaguely.

"I mean, I can't believe the shop gave me a witch's hat back!" Sophie grumbled.

"Right . . ."

"I just took it there because the brim was fraying," said Sophie. "I should have just fixed it myself. I'm sure they sold the sorcerer's hat to someone else."

"The hat! You're looking for the sorcerer's hat!" said Uma.

Sophie was suddenly not as friendly. She frowned. "Yeah, and you said you had it."

"Pointy blue one? With all those stars and moons on it?

What's so special about it?" asked Uma. She would never understand the ways of wizards.

"Nothing!" said Sophie abruptly.

"Nothing?" said Uma suspiciously.

"The professor doesn't like to be without it," Sophie finally admitted. "He's a little sensitive about his bald spot."

Uma raised an eyebrow. "That can't be all it is."

"Fine! Whoever wears the hat is able to use his power, except there's no magic on the Isle, thankfully," said Sophie. "But I still need to get it back. So, out with it. Do you have it or not?"

Uma slammed a palm on the table. "Of course I have it! And it can be yours *if*—"

"What do you mean *if*?" asked Sophie.

"If you give me something in return," said Uma with a wicked smile. "Can't get something for nothing, you know. Ursula's rule. And you're on our turf now."

Sophie's eyes narrowed. "What do you want for it?"

"Tell me where Yen Sid keeps my mother's necklace," said Uma.

"You want Ursula's necklace?" asked Sophie.

"Are you deaf? Yes, I want her necklace—the seashell one!" growled Uma.

"But it's broken; what would you need it for . . . ?" said Sophie.

"I don't care, I want it. It was my mother's, and I want it back," said Uma. "Sentimental value, shall we say."

"You? Sentimental? As if!"

"It was my mother's!" said Uma. "It's rightfully mine."

Sophie stuck her nose in the air. "Be that as it may, it's the property of the kingdom now. It belongs in the museum," she said in a superior tone. "The only reason it's still on the Isle is—"

"The embargo," said Uma. "I know."

"I'm not telling you where it is," said Sophie.

"Fine, then no hat," said Uma.

"You don't have it," said Sophie.

Uma grunted in frustration and motioned for backup.

"Sophie," said Harry, stepping up to the table from the shadows. "You're surrounded. There are many of us and only one of you, and you don't have any magic at your disposal. You're going to lose. We don't want to hurt you. But we could."

She trembled. "I'm not afraid."

Uma glared at her. "You should be."

"Okay, so if I tell you where the necklace is, you'll give me the sorcerer's hat back," said Sophie.

"Precisely." Harry smiled and nonchalantly wiped his hook on the front of his shirt, so she could see how sharp it was.

"I can't tell you where it is," said Sophie. "I just can't."

"Why not? I'll give you whatever you desire," said Uma, trying a different tack.

"How? There's no magic on the island, and last I checked

you're not Ursula, and I don't need to sell you my voice for a pair of legs."

"Not interested in princes, are you?" said Uma.

"Princes are boring. Have you even met Chad Charming? That's all you need to know," said Sophie.

"There are other things a girl might want. I don't need magic to help you," said Uma. "Tell me, there's got to be something you need that you can't have. A way out of your internship? A better apartment down at the Knob? Maybe even another date with Gil? Pirates over princes every time, am I right?"

Sophie shook her head. Uma and Harry exchanged a look and left the table—Uma ostensibly to serve other customers; Harry had no excuse but followed Uma anyway. "She won't budge," said Uma.

"You're losing your touch," said Harry.

"Oh, stuff it," said Uma. "You couldn't get her to spill either."

Harry shrugged. "The Uma I know could talk the hat off a wizard."

"If only we had the sorcerer's hat," said Uma. "Or if we could come up with something else she wants that I can give her."

"Or else?" said Harry, holding up his hook with a wicked grin.

"If it comes down to that, yes. But hold on."

Uma returned to the table empty-handed. "I don't think you have it," said Sophie, taking a last sip of her drink and gathering her things.

"Are you sure?" Uma smiled mysteriously.

Sophie hesitated, considering the odds. "I'm pretty sure. . . ." She crossed her arms over her chest and seemed to have come to a decision. "We're done here," she said, getting up. "Tell Gil next time he should take me to the Slop Shop instead."

"Wait, where are you going?" roared Uma.

"Home," said Sophie. "I don't need anything from you but the sorcerer's hat, and you don't have it."

"How can you be so sure?"

"Because. I've looked everywhere and so has Professor Yen Sid. If we can't find it, no one can." She regarded Uma with hostility. "Just admit you don't have it already!"

"But I do!" said Uma.

"Prove it!" said Sophie.

"I will!" said Uma hotly, annoyed to be questioned. She stood from the table, her mind racing. Sophie mentioned losing it in a hat shop, which rang a bell. . . . Why? Where had she seen a hat like the sorcerer's? She knew she'd spotted it somewhere. . . . But where?

Then she remembered.

"Gil!" she said, finding him throwing darts at the poster of King Ben on the wall. "Do you have those hats you bought from the shop the other day?"

"I do!" said Gil with a big smile. "But you said they didn't look good on me."

"I don't need you to wear them, I need you to bring them back here."

Gil ran off and came back carrying a big sack. "This one?" he said, showing her his white cowboy hat. "Or this one?" He held up a black top hat.

"No, the pointy one," said Uma impatiently.

Gil reached into the bag once more and before he could say anything, Uma had already grabbed it out of his hand.

Uma ran back to the table, holding the pointy velvet hat aloft. "Is this what you're looking for?" she asked Sophie triumphantly.

"Where on earth did you find it?" said Sophie, shocked and happy.

"Bought it at the hat shop, of course," said Uma, dangling the hat with the tips of her fingers and walking dangerously close to the open flame in the center of the room. "Now tell me where Yen Sid is hiding my mother's necklace. Or I'll throw it into the fire."

chapter
20

Desert Pride

Since the Great Wall blocked the direct way to the desert kingdom, Ben and Lonnie had to take the jet, despite the short distance of the trip. Ben could see why the people of Agrabah insisted on the flying carpets. Without air rights in the area, they'd have to go completely out of their way to get to Stone City. Once they set foot in Agrabah, they were met with as much fanfare and joy on that side as in the village.

The Sultan's nephew, the Grand Vizier, awaited them at the bottom of the mountain. While it had been cold and damp in Stone City, Ben found he was already sweating in his regiment coat after a minute in the hot desert sun.

"Welcome, welcome!" said the Grand Vizier, walking toward them with his arms outstretched, the golden bells decorating his elaborately embroidered sandals tinkling with every step. Like the citizens of Northern Wei, residents of Agrabah wore both traditional and modern garb; the Grand Vizier wore a shiny tracksuit and a pair of noise-reducing headphones around his neck. He embraced them warmly and kissed them on both cheeks, in keeping with the native custom.

The Sultan's people kept watch over the royal jet while the Grand Vizier led them toward a pair of camels for their journey to the palace. The desert kingdom hadn't changed much from the days when Aladdin prowled the souk in the middle of the city with his pet monkey. The place was buzzing with merchants and tourists haggling with each other, arguing over the prices of spices and rugs.

Ben found the camel ride a bit bumpy, but soon enough they were sitting comfortably on rugs in the Grand Vizier's great room, while a succession of mouthwatering dishes were presented for their nourishment—lamb tagine with stewed prunes and apricots, great bowls of couscous, eggplant turnovers, and aromatic saffron rice.

"Is this our third lunch?" Lonnie asked, amused at all the feasting the trip had brought.

"I stopped counting," said Ben, piling his plate high with food from every dish presented in front of him.

"How are things in Stone City?" asked the Grand Vizier,

when they had finished eating. "I know you stopped there first. I hope you have time to listen to our side of this sorry tale."

"I do have time, that's why I'm here," said Ben, taking a sip of sweet-smelling tea served in an ornate silver cup. "I understand it's a question of air rights over the Great Wall in regard to the use of flying carpets."

"Yes," said the Grand Vizier, his face darkening. "The Great Wall keeps us out of Stone City, and so the flying carpets are our only means of transport to reach what has always been a trading partner for us."

"I understand," said Ben.

"And they've told you about our olive situation as well, yes? Our farmers plant and nurture the trees, but the wind carries the fruit over the wall, and the imperials are the ones who benefit from our hard work. Now I ask you, is that fair?"

Ben demurred from answering just yet.

"The leaves from the trees also blow over to the Stone City, and they have to clean it up," said Lonnie hotly. "Agrabah doesn't offer to help clean up the mess, but only demands the villagers return the fruit without payment."

"We don't have to pay for something we create ourselves!" said the Grand Vizier, just as hotly.

Lonnie jumped to her feet, a hand on her sword. The Grand Vizier did the same, a hand on his scimitar, and the guards in the room followed suit, ready to attack on the Grand Vizier's command.

"Now, now," said Ben, holding out his hands in a pacifying gesture. "We don't have to fight. We're here to find some peace between the two kingdoms. You have both been good neighbors for centuries, and you can still continue to be good neighbors for centuries more."

"What is your solution?" asked the Grand Vizier.

"A compromise," said Ben, trying to catch Lonnie's eye. But she was looking at her feet, seemingly still angry at the Grand Vizier.

"Compromise?" said the Grand Vizier, shaking his head. "There is no compromise. We need to fly our carpets! And we want our olives back! Nothing else!"

"Grand Vizier, what would it take for you to listen to my proposed solution?" asked Ben.

The Grand Vizier shook his head, and it appeared all hopes of a truce had disappeared, when Lonnie unexpectedly knelt before the Grand Vizier like a supplicant, and offered him her sword, holding it lengthwise and balanced on the edge of her fingertips. "Forgive me, Grand Vizier, for my rudeness earlier," she said, her head bowed low.

The Grand Vizier looked shocked. "The imperial favorite's daughter, bowing to me?"

"Yes, my lord," said Lonnie, her eyes on the floor. "I took advantage of your hospitality and should never have acted in such a hostile manner in your presence. Normally I wouldn't do something like that. I'm not sure what came over me, but my mother taught me that honor is about admitting when you are wrong, and I was wrong."

The Grand Vizier looked thoughtful for a moment. "I accept your apology," he said. "Please, rise."

Lonnie stood up. Ben tensed, wondering what was going to happen now. But the Grand Vizier smiled kindly. It appeared he had been moved by Lonnie's humble gesture.

"I will listen to you, King of Auradon," he said. "Because if someone of such high imperial blood can admit their mistake, the people of Agrabah are not so proud that we cannot do the same. Perhaps we can work with them as we have before."

"I am glad to hear it," said Ben, grateful that Lonnie had insisted she come along on this task and proud that she had changed the mind of the Grand Vizier without having to resort to battle—even if she had acted a bit more rashly than he'd had in mind.

"If you please, tell me the Auradon compromise," said the Grand Vizier. "I find I am quite excited to hear it."

Ben took a deep breath and explained his idea. Now all he had to do was convince everyone that his solution was the answer to their problem.

chapter
21

Thieves in the Night

"Who's down here?" asked Fairy Godmother, holding her wand high in the air like a torch and walking closer and closer to the speedboat.

"Quick, hide!" said Mal, and the four of them scrambled to find the nearest hiding place. Jay and Carlos dove under the seats, while Mal and Evie crouched behind a few containers.

"Do you think she saw us?" Carlos whispered worriedly. His heart was pounding rapidly under his black-and-white leather jacket.

"I hope not," said Mal, crouching down even lower in the shadows.

"I swear I heard something," said Fairy Godmother, sending beams of light everywhere.

The light arced over the boat they were hiding in, but no one moved, so it danced over to the next boat. Carlos breathed a small sigh of relief.

"I guess I was wrong," muttered Fairy Godmother, and she walked back toward the shuttered yacht club at the end of the dock and began waving her wand again, making the windows sparkle and giving the building a new coat of paint.

"What's Fairy Godmother doing down here anyway?" Evie whispered.

"It looks like she's working on the royal yacht club," said Mal. "Ben's parents are returning from their cruise, and I think that's where they're planning to hold the welcome reception. I heard the work on getting the place up to snuff was behind schedule."

"How long is she going to be here? My legs are getting cramped," complained Jay.

"Shush!" said Mal.

They watched as Fairy Godmother unfurled giant banners with the Auradon crest and gave the yacht club sign a little more sparkle.

"There," said Fairy Godmother. "That should do it." She began walking away from the dock and back to the harbor entrance.

Carlos found he could breathe again. If they'd been caught stealing the royal speedboat, they would be in so much trouble. It felt as if his stomach had dropped into his shoes ever since he heard their headmistress's voice.

Mal poked her head up to check, and there was no sign of Fairy Godmother anywhere. "I think she's gone," she said, stepping out from behind the boat's containers. The rest of them came out from their hiding places, Evie hugging herself with her arms and Carlos still looking uncertain. Only Jay appeared unfazed.

"Let's give it a little more time," suggested Evie.

"Good idea," said Carlos, who was not in any rush to get moving.

They waited a little while longer, sitting in the dark and listening to the waves slosh gently against the sides of the boat. When Mal was satisfied Fairy Godmother had left the harbor, she nodded to the team.

"Okay, let's go," she said, tapping the steering wheel as she muttered the words of the spell, and the boat's engine roared to life once more.

Alas, a second later, the entire dock was flooded with light, and this time, Fairy Godmother caught them boat-handed.

"Aha! I knew there was someone here!" said Fairy Godmother triumphantly. She walked down the narrow dock, pointing her wand at the perpetrators. "Mal, Jay, Carlos, and Evie! What are you four doing down here? And with the royal speedboat?" She gasped. "Are you *stealing* it?"

It certainly looks that way, thought Carlos.

"Fairy Godmother! We can explain!" said Mal.

"Yes! We were, uh . . ." said Carlos, as he vainly tried to come up with a plausible explanation as to why they had trespassed onto the royal dock.

But Fairy Godmother shook her head, her lips a tight line. She kept the wand trained on the four of them and herded them away from the shoreline. "Shush, I don't want to hear it till we're safely back at school!"

She bundled all the four villain kids into her van and drove them to Auradon Prep. They sat in silence in the backseats, miserable and scared.

"What do you think's going to happen to us?" whispered Carlos from the third row.

"A lot of detention?" Mal whispered back. "That can't be too bad, right? We'll just have to bake a lot of cakes?"

"Hopefully she won't send us back to the Isle of the Lost," said Jay.

Evie squeaked. "She wouldn't do that, would she?"

"She could," said Mal.

"Oh no," said Evie. "I don't want to go back there."

"But it's home," said Mal, trying to soothe her friend. "It won't be that bad."

"Mal, don't you understand? Auradon is my home now," said Evie, looking out the window at the array of lights from the sparkling castles that dotted the landscape.

Carlos nodded. He couldn't go back to the Isle of the Lost, not after everything they'd seen and done in Auradon.

The thought filled him with a heavy dread. He couldn't go back to scrubbing his mother's bunions. He wouldn't.

"No talking back there!" said Fairy Godmother from the driver's seat. "And no talking on your phones either!" With a flick of her wand, all their phones disappeared.

When they got back to campus, Fairy Godmother marched them in front of her, holding the wand at Jay's back at the end of the line. The hallways were full of students heading to dinner. Carlos thought longingly of his life in Auradon, convinced this was the end of the tale. He hadn't even been able to say goodbye to Dude. The school would not look kindly on thievery. Or was it grand larceny? Marine larceny? Worse, it was exactly what the good people of Auradon expected from a few villain kids. Except they weren't villains anymore, not at all, and they were only stealing the boat so they could help a friend. But what was that saying? About the path to darkness? It was paved with good intentions. . . .

A few students looked at them curiously, but no one said hello, as Fairy Godmother had a very angry look on her usually cheerful face.

One student wasn't deterred, however—Jane spotted them on the way to Fairy Godmother's office.

"Mom!" she said, stopping in her tracks. "What's going on?"

Carlos's heart lurched once more, this time with hope.

Maybe Fairy Godmother would listen to Jane! Jane could make her understand they weren't doing something evil.

He was about to answer her, but Fairy Godmother didn't give him a chance. "Nothing, dear, get out of the way," said Fairy Godmother, brushing off her only child, and striding to the front of the pack. "This doesn't concern you."

But Jane wouldn't be dismissed so easily. She fell in step with the four friends. "What happened?" asked Jane. "Why's my mom so mad?"

Jay looked glum. Mal shook her head. "I don't want to get you in trouble too," she said.

"Evie? What's wrong? Are you crying?" asked Jane, as they kept walking up the stairs.

Evie sniffled but didn't answer.

They reached the landing and Fairy Godmother unlocked the door to her office. She tapped her wand and motioned the villain kids to enter.

Jane caught Carlos's sleeve before he disappeared behind the door. "Carlos? What's the matter? What did you guys do?"

"Help us," Carlos whispered urgently. "I think we're going to be kicked out of here."

"Kicked out?" said Jane, so aghast that she almost dropped her books. She stared at Carlos, shocked and wide-eyed at the very idea. "But you guys can't leave!"

"We don't want to," he said, feeling as terrible as he looked.

"I'll figure out something, I promise," said Jane. "You guys aren't going anywhere."

He smiled his thanks and reached for her hand. Jane gave it a squeeze, but had to let go as Fairy Godmother pulled Carlos into the room.

It was too bad their little Auradon experiment was ending already, thought Carlos. He would have really liked to spend more time in Jane's company.

chapter

22

A Pirate's Life

Outside on the dock, Harry was gathering the pirates together, slapping backs, readying the crew for the voyage ahead. Their merry band was ready, polishing swords and greedy for treasure. Once they found that trident and they were off the Isle of the Lost, there was all of Auradon to pillage! The thought brought them all much wicked glee.

"I heard in Agrabah there are warehouses full of the Sultan's gold," said Desiree.

"Don't forget the jewels we'll find in the Summerlands by the dwarf mines," growled Gonzo, his eyes going starry at the thought.

"Olympus is mine!" said Bonny.

Pirates. Harry smiled. They were itching for adventure. First, the trident; after, the world was theirs for the taking.

Inside, from the window of her small apartment above the fish shop, Uma felt a grim satisfaction as she looked at her reflection in the mirror. The time had come. It was so close, she could feel it—this was the start of her revenge, the start of her ascendancy. No more tiny room, no more apartment drenched in fish stink. She didn't need a fancy limousine to fetch her off the island, she would do it herself, cut her own deal, make her own way.

"I'm leaving, Ma!" she yelled, and a slender blue tentacle crept around from behind the door and splashed her with a few drops of water. It was the only goodbye she expected, the only one she needed. She was off to find herself; her past would soon be nothing more than a memory.

She clambered down the stairs, saying goodbye to it all: to that step that wobbled, and that patch of mold that could never be washed from the ceiling corner. She strode through the door and out onto the dock. Her ship lay waiting; the crew snapping to attention when she arrived in their midst.

Uma regarded them with pride. Just that morning she'd had nothing but slow-burning frustration and a jealous rage. But tonight she had so much more—she was captain of a ship, with a first mate and muscle to boot, as well as a crew of the toughest pirates on the island. Her name was Uma, and before long, everyone in Auradon would know who she was when she lifted that trident and demanded her freedom.

The first part of her plan had already worked perfectly. Sophie had crumbled like a piece of cake once Uma had threatened to set fire to the sorcerer's hat, and she had given up the necklace's secret location as soon as the flames had licked the brim.

"Ready?" Uma asked Harry.

In response, Harry gave her the usual pirate salute— which was no salute at all. He cocked an eyebrow and grinned. "Ready." He raised his hook, which had been polished to a high shine. It gave him an air of malevolence that she quite liked.

"Gil?" she said.

"Yes, Shrim—Uma," said Gil. "And, um, do you think we can grab dinner after this? I'm hungry."

"Let's go," said Uma, ignoring him and leading the way.

The motley crew headed down the wharf toward the *Lost Revenge*. They shambled past the rope bridge and toward the decks of the pirate ship, setting about unfurling the sails, hoisting up the jib, and removing the ropes that held it to the deck so it would be ready for launch.

Uma climbed the steps of the forecastle and turned to face the heavy wooden rail. The foremast stood at her back, ropes flanking her on two sides. The crew gathered on the main deck. The ship was ready to sail.

She drew her sword from its scabbard, the blade flashing

yellow and orange in the evening light. This was her crew, her people. Time to put them in order. "Pirates! Somewhere on the Isle of the Doomed is a treasure chest that holds the pieces of a necklace that belonged to my mother! If we find it, I can call that fool Triton's trident from the sea and use it to win our freedom from this island prison! Are you with me?"

"*Arrrr!*" cried the pirates. A few grunts followed and a shrug or two. In pirate terms, it was a good enough reception.

Uma slashed the air with her sword. "We ride with the tide!" she cried.

"We ride with the tide!" roared Harry, raising his sword just as high.

"We ride with the tide?" said Gil. He shrugged his shoulders, removed his cutlass, and waved it in the air like the rest of them. The rest of the pirates joined in, raising their blades and cheering in unison.

Harry took hold of the wheel and kicked off the motor that would power the ship until the wind took hold. The *Lost Revenge* solemnly pulled out of the dock and into the dark waters beyond. A curious crowd gathered by the harbor to watch as it pulled away, some tossing rotten tomatoes at the ship's bow in the usual Isle send-off.

Harry steered the ship out past the shattered lighthouse, and through the fog he could make out the barrier over the Isle of the Lost and the waters surrounding it. But they had room to move, and when they reached the Strait of Ursula, the wind blew and the sails plumped at last. But the ocean waves were choppy and high, slamming the ship's hull. They ran right into one, sending a spray of water onto deck, but Harry laughed as he peered through the mist and the crew seemed to take it all in stride.

At last, they were off.

Uma smiled, for once utterly gratified with how her life had turned out. She had her ship and her crew, and they were sailing to find their freedom.

chapter
23

Sail Away

Contentment didn't last long. "Um, Harry? Is this as fast as we can go?" she asked. The *Lost Revenge* had only sailed a few yards, and the dock was still in view. They had inched up the archipelago, but were still miles from where they needed to be. She paced the deck impatiently. First the necklace, and then the trident was theirs for the taking, if only they could get there faster.

"It only goes as fast as the wind will take it," said Harry. "Sorry."

"Right," said Uma. "I get it: the wind hits the sails and off we go." She looked up at the billowing white cloth. A single swatch of linen fluttered in the wind, held there by four ropes and tied to the foremost mast. But just behind it were not just one but two others. "What do you call those other masts?" she asked, acting a bit coy.

"Oh, yes," he replied, a bit sheepish, "that's the mainmast just behind the foremast, and the one in the back is called the mizzen."

"I see. And these masts have sails as well?" she asked, still acting coy. The boy had to know exactly where this was going, right? He told her he knew how to sail, didn't he?

"Yes, I mean technically we do have three masts," he allowed.

"And each one has a sail or two?"

"Three, actually."

"So why in the world aren't we using them all!" she yelled.

"Well, it's the waves, you see; with all of this rocking it would be quite difficult—no, dangerous, to go up there and unfurl the rest of the sails."

"So you're telling me we could be going two, three times this speed, and all we have to do is climb up there and unroll the rest of the sails?"

"Something like that," said Harry. "It's not as easy as it sounds. Try climbing fifty feet into the air while the boat is pitching to and fro, and see if you can hold on. These things—"

"I think I will." She was headed toward the second mast before he could make any further attempt to dissuade her from climbing it and wrestling with the sails.

How hard can it be? she thought. *Climb the mast, untie some ropes, and it's done.*

She looked at Harry with disdain as she raised her foot and caught hold of the first peg. She grabbed one and then another, and soon she was seven, eight feet in the air. The ship rolled and her face promptly collided with the mast; her hand slipped from one peg, her leg from the other, and she reeled. Were it not for that fact that her shirt had caught on yet another of the pegs she would have fallen onto the deck. Or worse, she might have landed in the ocean itself.

Harry snickered.

"I suppose this is that moment when you mutter *I told you so?*" she asked.

"I might have," said Harry. "But now you've gone and ruined it. I suppose I'll have to come up there and help you out. It does take two to unfurl a sail. You know that, don't you?"

She didn't. She hadn't the faintest idea of how any of this worked. She only wanted to get to the trident as quickly as was possible, and if that meant a bit of mast-climbing, she'd do it. She'd already made it past the hard part, right?

The boat leaned again, answering her question. This time she was ready, though, and wrapped her arms tightly around the mast. She wasn't going to let her feet slide from the pegs a second time.

Harry was snickering again.

She had half a mind to stab him when he reached her.

He held one peg tightly, balancing himself. "You're going to squeeze that mast in two if you hold on to it any tighter," he said.

She immediately loosened her grip and regained her composure.

"So tell me how all of this works," she ordered. Each time the ship rocked, the mast swayed wildly, hurtling them through the air. *Like being launched from a slingshot,* she thought, her hands wrapping a bit more tightly around the pegs again. At this height, there were rope ladders too—a great number of ropes actually, all of them running back and forth between the mast's various arms. There was more to grab on to, more to catch if she fell. She supposed she was a little safer at this altitude, but who knew.

"See that rope?" Harry pointed to a tightly wound bit of cord. "Unwrap it on your side, and I'll do the same on mine. Just hold the last little bit. Don't let the whole thing loose . . ." he said, but she had already unwound the rope. It was easy enough. She simply pulled the rope from the sail and cast it off.

Unfortunately, Harry hadn't even started to unfurl his end of the sail. So the end she had set free caught the wind, jerking the boat toward its starboard side, which was a boating term that Harry would not stop using. *Isn't it just called the right side?* she had thought over and over again, but now the word was in her head and *she* was using it.

"This would have been a bit easier if you had waited," Harry said grumpily.

"Got that," she said. The boat was turning rapidly to one side, threatening to pull them off course, but Harry was quick, his fingers nimble. The sail pulled at the ropes, tightening them, but somehow he managed to get the rope unwound, and the entire sail billowed gorgeously into the air.

The ship righted itself.

"Next time we do it together!" he exclaimed, and Uma made no argument. She was eager to get to the necklace and the trident, but she'd already twice seen where a bit of overeagerness got her. She'd nearly fallen into the drink (as pirates called the sea) and partially driven them off course. *I think it's time to listen to directions,* she thought.

Uma *hated* directions. She gave orders; she didn't follow them.

But she climbed to the next sail as Harry directed. This one had a plank behind it and a rail, so it was easier to balance as she undid the ropes.

"Wait," said Harry.

"I know. I'm not an idiot."

He raised an eyebrow.

"Now!" he cried, and they both let loose the next sail. This one blossomed into a perfect half circle, snapping tight in the wind. They undid one more and then moved to the rear, where there were three more sails to unfurl. All in all, it was a lot of work, but each time a sail caught the wind, she felt their speed increase. By the time they'd unfurled the last of them, they were moving at quite a clip—the boat dashing across the waves, sometimes almost skipping from peak to peak.

"See, that wasn't so bad," she said as they climbed down the last mast, the *mizzenmast*, as he'd called it.

"You did nearly fall into the ocean," Harry reminded Uma. "Twice."

The boat rocked once more, as if it too were reminding her of what happened. It swung back in the other direction, and both of them spun, catching each other and holding on to the mast to avoid falling to the deck. The increased speed had also added a bit more instability to their ride, making it slightly more dangerous. When the boat rocked, it did so with incredible force. It pitched again, and even Harry went fumbling for something to hold on to. Fortunately, sailing ships are webbed with ropes. He caught one or two and steadied himself.

"Lost your sea legs?" Uma asked.

"Even a good sailor needs a handhold every now and then."

She nodded as if she didn't believe a word he'd said.

"Oh, stop it—don't we have a treasure chest to find?" Harry pointed out.

They did. She'd almost forgotten about it.

Uma stared out over the ocean. She knew the trident

was there, and she also knew she was not the only one looking for it. But they were moving faster now, and she had to
hope that they would find it first.

"That's all the sails?" she asked.

"That's it. I can throw an oar in the water if you want
to paddle?"

"I'll let you do that," she replied.

"I'm sailing this ship," Harry said—and indeed he
was moving back and forth, checking all of the ropes that
wound from the gunwale to the masts, from mast to mast
and from mast to sail. And all the while he had to make certain the rudder was set in the right direction. He'd fastened
it in place with a lash, but it needed constant correction. "If
you don't head straight into these waves they can knock you
over, leaving you on your side. And then you're done," he
said. "The sea is growing rougher: the waves are certainly
higher, and the wind's stronger. I hope this trident of yours
is worth all this effort."

"It is—trust me," said Uma. "With that trident, we can
buy our ticket out of here."

Harry shrugged. "I hope so. We're all counting on it."

chapter

24

Building a Compromise

"You think this will work?" asked Lonnie, as she and Ben watched a group of strongmen from Agrabah take sledgehammers to the Great Wall. The stone crumbled underneath their blows, and soon enough, there was a hole big enough to see through to the other side, where a similar group of imperial soldiers was doing the same thing.

"I hope so," said Ben, waving to Charlie, who waved back from his part of the wall.

When the hole was big enough to walk through, Ben crossed from the desert kingdom into Northern Wei's territory, the Grand Vizier by his side.

"Welcome to Stone City," said Charlie, bowing to the Grand Vizier.

"It is an honor to be here," said the Grand Vizier, bowing low as well. The two shook hands, and Charlie motioned for the group to take a seat on his porch, where they could watch the construction from a safe distance.

Ben had sent a pigeon to carry a message over the wall after he had convinced the Grand Vizier of his plan. Charlie then forwarded the message to the Emperor for approval. The Imperial City had sent its response—a white dove that meant the plan was approved.

And so, for the first time in the history of the Great Wall, there was going to be a door to Stone City on the other side. The people of Agrabah would no longer need to fly their carpets over the wall in order to get access, and the people of Stone City would no longer be aggravated by the noise from the pesky things.

"After all, we are not enemies," said Charlie. "We are neighbors and friends, and have been for thousands of years. The wall was built for one purpose, but now must serve another."

"Not enemies at all," agreed the Grand Vizier, slurping his bubble tea and chewing noisily on the tapioca balls. "What *is* this amazing concoction?"

Charlie explained the provenance and the ingredients that went into the making of bubble tea, and the Grand Vizier declared he would press the Sultan to serve it during their festival, which was coming up in a month or so.

Ben laughed, glad to see that the dispute had been resolved amicably.

The two kingdoms also agreed that the olive trade would be overseen by foremen from both sides of the wall, and that the Stone City and Agrabah would both take care of harvesting the olives and pruning the trees. The desert farmers even offered to teach the villagers how to nurture and care for the trees, and in turn the villagers offered to trade recipes and other spices. A few Stone City farmers even suggested planting olive trees on their side of the wall, although the Grand Vizier told Ben in confidence that he wasn't sure that was a feasible idea, since the climates of the two kingdoms differed greatly. Olive trees were a desert fruit, and the Stone City's mountainous terrain would not be conducive to its flowering. But who knew? Ben reminded them they lived in Auradon after all, where the impossible had a way of becoming possible: where street rats married Sultans' daughters, and awkward girls grew up to be great warriors.

Ben and Lonnie bade their goodbyes to Charlie and the Grand Vizier. "You must come visit us again, especially during harvest season," said Charlie.

"I will."

"See you at the Agrabah Festival," said the Grand Vizier.

"I look forward to it."

"And thank you again, young lady, for being brave

enough to change an old man's mind," said the Grand Vizier to Lonnie.

Lonnie bowed low in appreciation.

"They're bringing your horses now," said Charlie. "Safe journey back."

Ben thanked them again, and watched as Charlie and the villagers retired to their side of the wall and the Grand Vizier and his entourage exited to their side. But a few workers from both cities stayed at the site, finishing up the construction of the Great Wall's first Great Door.

"Where did you get the idea to apologize like that?" Ben asked Lonnie, when their new friends were out of earshot.

"From my mother," said Lonnie. "I realized not every dispute has to be resolved with a sword. She said that sometimes a good apology can also do the trick. Mushu is always apologizing, by the way."

"Of course he is," said Ben, chuckling.

They headed toward the royal jet, when all of a sudden a strange whirlwind surrounded Ben.

"Don't be afraid!" a voice boomed. "Just stay still."

"Ben?" Lonnie called fearfully. "What's happening?"

"I don't know," he replied, as the whirlwind around him twirled faster and faster. "But I think it's okay." He recognized that voice, so he remained still and wondered where this next journey would take him.

chapter
25

Doom and Gloom

"Foggy," said Harry, as he steered the ship away from the Isle of the Lost and toward the Isle of the Doomed, where the treasure chest containing Ursula's necklace was supposed to be buried. "I don't recall ever seeing this much fog in the bay."

"Do you think it's a bad sign?" asked Uma, who was still perched against the rail, gazing out at the bowsprit. A gorgeously carved mermaid adorned the long wooden pole. Sculpted with almost lifelike detail, it was painted in shades of teal and coral, the colors of the sea.

"I don't think it's any sign at all. Sometimes a fog is just a fog." Harry shrugged.

"I'm sure you're right, but it still gives me the chills. I know there's no magic here, but it's not much of a start. How we will navigate through all this fog?" Uma asked. They had sailed into a dense patch of gray. It was all around them, on their arms and in their noses. It left a cool, damp feeling on her face, like cold perspiration.

"I don't mind, and there are many ways to sail in the fog. Leave the navigation to me," Harry continued. "There are far worse things in the sea than a gray sky. Try sailing through ten-foot waves or one-hundred-mile-an-hour winds."

"I see your point."

Harry was trying to sound optimistic. He was the one with the sea legs. He wasn't supposed to be afraid, not out here. But it wasn't the sea that bothered him. Their destination was another matter. The Isle of the Doomed wasn't exactly a paradise. That was probably why Yen Sid had hidden the broken necklace in a treasure chest on the smaller island in the first place. No one from the Isle of the Lost ever visited the Isle of the Doomed—not if they could help it. It was rumored to be haunted, and Maleficent's fortress loomed, tall and forbidding, over its desolate landscape. The island's only inhabitants were the descendants of goblins loyal to the evil fairy. *There must be some reason they call it the Isle of the Doomed*, Harry thought. But he wasn't sure he wanted to find out what it was—or if the rumors he heard about it were true.

Even with the fog, they sailed smoothly. The winds were light, but the ship moved at a respectable clip, cutting through the waves, edging ever closer to the shore.

"I wish the fog weren't so dense. I'd like to get a better sense of the beach before we set anchor. There could be rocks or . . ." said Harry. Then he stopped.

"What?" asked Uma.

"I don't know. This is a forbidden place. There could be anything hiding in those waters, and this fog isn't helping. There could be spikes—iron ones, submerged below the waterline—obstacles to keep boats from landing on the island. This might not be as easy as we expect, Uma."

Harry thought about what else could be out there. Goblins swarming over that beach, or traps, or who knows what. Anything could be hiding in a fog this thick.

"Let's stop here," Harry announced. "We'll drop anchor and row out in small boats. We'll make a smaller target, harder to spy on, and if there's anything in the water we'll be able to see it more easily."

Uma protested at first. She didn't like his suggestion. It would only slow things down. She was ready to be bold and take chances, and she told him so. But she went along with Harry, for now. "Fine," she said at last. "We'll do it your way."

So they rowed out with the crew in small wooden boats, hugging the sea, creeping toward the dark beach, their hulls grinding against the sand as they made shore. Uma was the first out of the boat, her feet falling into the cold water. It drenched her up to the knees. The sand here was gray, like the sky and the fog that still choked the air. Goblin Beach was dark and deserted, ghostly under the moonlight.

"At least it's empty. No goblins," said Uma.

"Not yet," Harry said.

"All right, Sophie said Yen Sid left some sort of clue, a trail," said Uma.

"Like a path?" asked Harry.

"Maybe, but I don't think it's anything that obvious," said Uma. "I'm certain it's as hidden as the chest itself." She eyed the distant fortress, tall and dark, its black stones wreathed in angry thorns. And she swore it glowed a strange color—something like purple, but at times it shifted, turning to shades of green, like the photos Uma had seen of the aurora borealis. But the colors were gone as soon as she glanced at it, vanishing as if they had never been there at all. "Let's head toward the castle."

"Are you sure?" said Harry. "That place is filled with goblins. We don't want those little guys to find out we're looking for something valuable, or they're bound to try and steal it."

"We're only heading toward it, dummy. I didn't say anything about crossing the moat."

"Good, as I'm more of a seafaring adventurer, less of an evil-castle explorer."

"We all are," mumbled Gil.

The pale sand of the fog-shrouded beach gave way to a forest of gray thorn-infested trees. Their trunks wound every which way, growing in seemingly unnatural patterns, curling in upon themselves or twisting into odd spirals, as if some mad gardener had tortured them, forcing their limbs to twist into tangled bunches. It made for slow going, and more than once Harry was forced to draw his cutlass and hack through the thorns and the trees. Even the ferns were dense, and he hacked at those as well.

"At least there's no goblins," he said as he slashed at a thorn tree, slicing clear through its base, sending it tumbling to the side. The dense forest at the shoreline thinned as they drove deeper into it. It soon cleared, and they were walking around in low grass. Harry sheathed his blade.

"Now that Harry has graciously led us through the thorns, I think we can spread out," said Uma.

"What do we do if we find anything?" asked Harry.

"Just yell," said Uma, brazen as ever.

"But that might draw the attention of you-know-what." He eyed the imposing fortress.

"Live a little," said Uma. "And quit your worrying. "We've come this far, haven't we?"

Gil *humphed*, and Harry rolled his eyes.

The crew dispersed, fanning out in all directions— eager to search for treasure, but always aware of the fortress, which seemed to watch over them, its tower looming in the distance.

Harry went toward what looked like a jungle. Desiree lingered at the thorny grove, while Uma and Gil headed toward the castle's base, where smaller trees grew amidst tumbled stones.

Harry hacked his way into the jungle. They were looking for a trail. Most of those were on the ground, he thought, but the earth here was covered in a thick layer of underbrush, and the trees grew so closely together he had to press each branch aside with his shoulders while he hacked at the ferns with his cutlass, his hook gathering up what was shorn and tossing it aside. Each time he cleared a patch of ferns or some other jungle plant, there was nothing resting beneath it—nothing that looked like a path, at least.

He turned to see if Uma and Gil had made any progress, but they had disappeared into the rocks. He wiped the sweat from his brow and wondered if this was all just a waste of time. The jungle was too dense; they'd never find a trail here. Maybe they needed a new strategy. He turned, following the path that he had already cut through the forest, hoping to find Uma and the others.

On his way back, he hacked at a particularly old and tangled branch, one he had pushed aside when he'd first come through. The branch fell, leaving a slender stump dangling from the face of the tree. There was a cut below the stump, and at first Harry mistook it for the stroke of his own blade. But he had been making slender cuts that went from side to side. This was something altogether different.

It was a carving. When the clouds cleared and a bit of light shone through the canopy, he noticed that it formed a distinct pattern.

"I've found something!" he called out, loudly but not too loudly, still concerned he might draw the goblins' attention. A moment passed. He glanced up at Maleficent's fortress, wondering if hundreds of the crafty little creatures were watching him.

chapter
26

Secrets and Lies

$\mathcal{M}$al shifted her weight from foot to foot as the four of them stood on the rug in Fairy Godmother's office, where just yesterday they had surrendered their evil talismans. They definitely weren't those heroes anymore. She had a sinking feeling in her stomach. This was the exact opposite of what she had intended to happen when she'd taken on Arabella's problem. She'd only meant to help a friend, but she'd gotten them all in trouble in the process.

"I'm sorry, guys," Mal whispered.

Evie put an arm around Mal. "It's okay."

"We're all in this together," said Jay. "We go down as one."

"I just hope we're not really going down," said Carlos.

Fairy Godmother finished locking the door and stood in front of the group. She stared at each of them in turn with a frosty glare. "What is the meaning of this? Outside of school property and past the security gate down at Belle's Harbor! The rules are there to keep you kids safe, you know."

Mal grimaced as Evie and Carlos looked chagrined, but Jay tried for a winning smile. "You see, Fairy G, we were—"

"Hush!" said Fairy Godmother, putting up her palm.

"We were just—" said Mal softly.

"Hush!" said Fairy Godmother again.

They all began to talk all at once. "We were night-swimming!" said Jay.

"We saw in the magic mirror that . . ." said Evie.

"Auradon is in danger," said Carlos.

"Uma can't win!" cried Mal.

"One at a time!" said Fairy Godmother.

Once again, they all started to speak at the same time.

"You go ahead," said Mal to Evie.

"No, you go," said Evie to Carlos.

"You explain," said Carlos to Jay.

"I will," said Jay. "Well, you see, Fairy G, it's like this . . ." he began.

"Stop," said Mal. "I know what you're about to say." Jay was an experienced and practiced liar, and no doubt he'd already come up with a good story and was fabricating some details in his mind.

"You do?" asked Jay.

"Whatever it is, it's not the truth. And I think we need to tell the truth tonight," said Mal, sticking her hands into her jacket pockets, her shoulders slumping in defeat.

"Are you sure?" said Jay.

"I would prefer the truth," said Fairy Godmother, sounding amused for the first time that evening.

"I'm sure," said Mal.

Fairy Godmother nodded. "Also, I must inform you that this is a very serious offense indeed. Stealing something that doesn't belong to you goes against every rule we have in Auradon. I'm afraid if you are found guilty of such a crime, you will all be expelled from Auradon Prep and sent back to the Isle of the Lost."

"Sent back!" cried Evie.

Carlos went pale.

Jay gulped.

Mal balled her hands into fists, frustrated. They were only trying to help. Uma was out there, and the trident was within her reach—not to mention that of all the other villains who were searching for it.

"So, yes, I dearly hope you have a good explanation for this." Fairy Godmother crossed her arms, still holding her wand like a weapon.

Maybe it was time to come clean, and confess all— Arabella's mischief, the missing trident, and their plan to recover it.

"You see, Fairy Godmother . . ." said Mal. She was just about to admit everything, when who should burst into the office but the King of Auradon himself.

Ben entered the room wearing a dusty regiment uniform, Jane at his heels. Before Mal could say anything more, Ben held up his hand. "What's going on here?" he asked. "Mal? What happened?"

"Oh! Ben," said Fairy Godmother. "I'm so glad you're here! We have a situation."

"I can see that," said Ben mildly. "Someone care to tell me what it is?"

"Fairy Godmother caught us in a restricted area by Belle's Harbor," said Mal. "On the royal speedboat."

"I see," said Ben, frowning.

"They were in the middle of stealing it," said Fairy Godmother, her voice rising an octave. "This is exactly what we feared when we let villains into Auradon."

I can explain, Mal mouthed when the headmistress wasn't looking.

Ben held his elbow with one hand and scratched his chin with the other. "Actually, Fairy Godmother, they were doing nothing of the sort. They weren't breaking any rules. They were down at the harbor because I sent them there."

"Right, we'll put them on the first boat back to the Isle of the Lost. . . . Wait, what?" said Fairy Godmother. "Excuse me? What did you say?"

"They weren't doing anything wrong. Mal, Evie, Jay, and

Carlos were on a secret mission for me, which is why they were on the royal speedboat. Because I told them to take it," said Ben firmly. "And that's why they couldn't explain what they were up to: because they knew it was confidential."

"They were on a secret mission for you? Did I hear that correctly?" Fairy Godmother cupped an ear.

Ben yelled into it. "Yes!" He exchanged a meaningful look with Mal.

"Ben, you don't have to do this," she whispered.

"Of course I do," he said. "I can't let you guys get in trouble when you were only doing this for me." He turned away before Fairy Godmother could get suspicious.

"See, Mom?" said Jane. "I told you they weren't doing anything wrong!"

"And may I ask what the secret mission is . . . ?" Fairy Godmother still looked unconvinced.

"Unfortunately it's council business," said Ben. "Top secret information that could compromise the safety of the kingdom. You do understand."

Fairy Godmother sighed and finally relented. "Of course. If you say so."

"You have my word," said Ben. He walked over to Mal and slung an arm around her shoulders. "I don't know what I was thinking, sending you guys on such a dangerous assignment alone. We'll do it together."

"I'm so sorry I meddled," said a contrite Fairy Godmother. "But I'm so relieved as well. I was quite distressed about expelling you," she told the four friends. "I couldn't believe my eyes when I found you."

"It's all right," said Jay with a grin.

"Don't worry, Fairy Godmother. All is well," said Ben.

"I'm glad to hear it. I hope I didn't disrupt your, um, mission," said Fairy Godmother, still mystified.

"Not at all," said Ben.

She turned to the four villain kids. "Well, then. It appears I owe you four an apology. I'm so sorry to have assumed the worst."

"Quite all right," said Evie. "It looked bad."

"So bad!" said Carlos.

"The very worst," said Jay. "Speedboats are expensive, aren't they?"

"We're sorry we couldn't tell you the truth," said Mal. "Are we dismissed?" she asked hopefully.

Fairy Godmother nodded. "If the king agrees," she said.

"I do," said Ben.

"Dismissed," said Fairy Godmother.

The six of them left the headmistress's office, but no one said a word until they were safely in Ben's study. Mal found she could breathe again when they were inside the plush, opulent suite, with its magnificent desk against the window and the gym equipment in the corner. Jay wiped his forehead and flopped down on the nearest couch. "Phew! That was close!"

"Too close," said Carlos, taking a seat next to him.

"I agree," said Evie. "Thanks for rescuing us, Ben."

"How'd you get back here so fast?" asked Mal.

"Jane called Merlin and told him to zap me back here immediately. At first, he was worried about using such dramatic magic, but she was able to convince him that it would be my wish given the circumstances," said Ben with a smile. "That felt weird, I've got to say. Not sure I have all my molecules back. Am I missing any part of me?" he asked, patting himself down.

"You look complete to me," said Mal, laughing in relief. She turned to Jane. "You are awesome," she said, giving Jane a quick hug.

"Thanks," said Jane, shrugging. "But I knew whatever it was my mother was mad about, it was probably just a misunderstanding. You guys can't be sent back to the Isle of the Lost!" Mal noticed Jane sneak a look at Carlos as she said this, and Carlos beamed.

"Did you get your work done, though?" Mal asked, turning to Ben. "Were you able to get the villagers on both sides of the wall to agree to the terms of the truce?"

"Yes, thanks to Lonnie," he said. "We were just about to return to Auradon when I was pulled away. She's taking the jet home in a bit. So fill me in. Why were you guys taking the boat in the first place?"

"It's my fault, I was the one who suggested we steal it. Never again," said Jay. "From now on, I'm going to follow every rule to the letter. I'm walking the straight and narrow path!"

"Well, now that we don't have to steal the boat, can we get back there, actually?" said Mal. "Ben, I'll fill you in on the way. But right now we've got a trident to find."

chapter
27

Treasure Hunt

*U*ma would never admit it, but the Isle of the Doomed gave her the creeps just as much as it did Harry. She'd lost him somewhere around the forest of thorns, but heard his call and made her way back to where she saw him last, finally coming upon him in the middle of a clearing.

"Tell me you've found the trail," she said, Gil right behind her.

"Nope, nothing like that," said Harry.

"Oh, so you got bored and gave up, did you?" she accused.

"Stop grouching. Follow me." Harry led them to what

he'd found. There, carved into the bark, a symbol glimmered in the evening light.

"What is it?" said Uma.

"A crescent," said Harry.

"Or maybe it's a moon," Gil added.

"A crescent *is* a moon," Harry snapped. He traced the mark with his finger. "The professor didn't make a map, Sophie said, because he thought it would be too dangerous to leave around. But he had to have some way to figure out where he'd kept it."

"You think this is it? This mark?" Uma asked.

"Shall I grab the shovels?" Gil asked.

"I don't think this symbol marks the treasure. Remember, we're looking for a trail. The path isn't on the ground. It's written on trees. If I'm right, there are more of these markings. Follow them, and we'll find the treasure," said Harry.

"Or we'll find out where two lovers carved a heart in some tree," said Uma.

"Are you trying to tell me something?" Harry joked.

"That I'll cut you if you don't find the treasure chest?" Uma snorted. "There's nothing here that says *trail* to me."

"Fine, you've got a better idea on how to find this thing?" Harry said.

Uma shook her head reluctantly. "It's just there are a lot of trees, and it's not exactly easy to get a look at their bark."

"I know, I had to hack off a branch to find this one, but

I think that's the point. The trail is hidden. It's not *supposed* to be easy to find."

And it wasn't. They searched trees and shrubs, rocks, and moss. They cut aside branches and sheared the leaves off of bushes.

"I'm beginning to feel like a lumberjack," Gil whined.

"And I'm—" Uma stopped.

"What is it?" Harry asked.

"About to give up. That was what I was going to say, but look here."

Her toe had hit a rock. A small sun—a rough circle, ringed by radiating lines—graced its surface. "I think our professor had a chisel," said Uma. "It's a sun, and I think that last one *was* a moon. This might be a trail after all," she said. Now her spirits were lifted. The impossible suddenly seemed a tad more possible, though they had found only two symbols. It wasn't exactly a trail, but it was a good enough start.

"Two points make a line," said Uma, "so let's look this way and that and see if there is another marker that aligns with these first two." She stood at a spot midway between the two marks and pointed in either direction. Gil went one way, Harry the other, hacking his way into the jungle as he went.

The third mark was easier to find than the second. It wasn't exactly in line with the first two, but it was close enough, so Harry found it relatively quickly.

"It's a star," said Uma when she caught up to him.

"We're on the right path," said Harry. "Three marks: the sun, the moon, and a star. Just like the symbols on the wizard's hat. It cannot be a coincidence."

As the crew drove deeper into the jungle, the marks were more difficult to unearth, hidden as they were among tangled branches or scratched on stones half covered by clumps of moss. And the trail bent in every direction, not following a straight line, but curving to and fro, making it difficult for the pirates to judge where they might find the next mark.

Branch after branch fell to the earth. Stones were overturned. They made a royal mess of the island, but there was no one there to complain about it. And Uma doubted the goblins would mind, although she still hoped they wouldn't notice all the noise. They followed the celestial markers. There were stars of all different types, and even a few constellations carved into the trees and rocks, but at last one symbol stood apart from the rest.

"This is it!" said Harry. He was kneeling in a clearing, brushing away some scattered leaves from the earth as Uma approached. Over his shoulder she read the words TOPS EHT SKRAM X deeply scrawled into the hard-packed dirt.

"Is it telling us to scram?" asked Harry, reading the text. "I do feel like getting out of here. That fortress gives me the creeps."

Uma shushed him. "It must be here. This is the spot. There's an *X*! Pirates love them. It's highly piratical."

"Yen Sid is a sorcerer, not a pirate. And this is a bit clichéd, if you ask me," Harry said.

"I didn't ask you," Uma replied, looking around, trying to discern what import the message held.

Harry stood and put away his sword.

Gil wandered over from the other side of the clearing and looked at the message upside down and backward. "'X MARKS THE SPOT'!" he declared.

"You're a genius!" said Harry.

"Let's not go that far," said Uma. "It's written backward. Even brats can figure out this code."

"But you guys didn't," Gil pointed out.

"Who cares? It was hard enough just finding this thing— let's start digging," said Harry, removing the shovel that he'd strapped to his back. He whistled for the rest of the crew, who came running, clanking through the jungle, picks and shovels at the ready. "We found it!" he told them. "Dig!"

"Where?" said Gil.

"On the *X*, just like it says," said Harry. "Makes sense, right?"

They dug, shoveling dirt and stone, and the pit grew larger and deeper. Harry and Gil were down in the hole as it grew in width as well as depth, but they didn't find a treasure chest.

"I knew this was too easy," said Harry as he climbed his way out of the hole. They had dug exactly on the spot the *X* had marked, but they'd found nothing. "There must be more to it. I mean, any random goblin could wander through the forest, find the *X*, and dig this thing up."

"You're right," Uma acknowledged. "The professor would never have done something so obvious. He hid his symbols well, so clearly he hid the chest just as well." She looked down at the symbol. "Wonder why he wrote the words backward. I mean, it's not much of a code."

"What if it's not a code?" Harry offered.

"What do you mean?"

"I mean, what if it's a direction of some sort," said Harry.

Gil was already ahead of them. He had turned around backward and walked to a place where two trees grew at strange angles. One tipped to the right and the other to the left. Together they formed an *X*.

"There it is!" Uma saw the *X* formed by the trees. If she turned so the hole was at her back, this tree was exactly in line with where the carving had been. So once more, they drew shovels and thrust them into the earth, digging as fast as they could.

chapter

28

Twisted Mysteries

*H*arry dug furiously by the X-shaped trees, forming a pit that was too small for anyone else to stand in when the sound of steel striking wood echoed in the hole. "I think I found it!" he crowed, his entire body covered with mud.

Uma ran to the edge of the pit, Gil at her shoulder. "You found it?" she asked, sounding as if she didn't quite believe it.

"I did!" he said, hitting the shovel on the ground again, this time with an extra-strong wallop. That was when the ground gave way underneath his feet and he tumbled down into the darkness.

Harry flailed in the air, barely hanging on to his hook. He was falling, the wind blowing in his face. He nearly retched. His stomach heaved. He was weightless and then he wasn't. With a great splash, he struck water. He had fallen a good distance, and he did not hit the water lightly.

"It might as well have been concrete," he mumbled, splashing around.

He was in a great underground lagoon, black as night and as still as ice on a frozen lake. Harry frantically tried to keep his head above water. A pair of light trousers and a thin shirt would have been useful in such circumstances, but pirates wore neither, and Harry's heavy clothes threatened to draw him down. He threw off his jacket and paddled to the shore. At least he *did* know how to swim.

Harry checked for injuries—water can break bones after a fall from such heights—but he was intact. His back stung from when he'd struck the surface, but that pain would fade. Only his pride was truly damaged—he'd landed in the ultimate belly flop. Luckily, no one had been around to see it.

His eyes slowly adjusted to the darkness, but there wasn't much to see. He could not even make out the far side of the lagoon. Harry looked up and found only an enveloping darkness.

He was trapped. "Help!" he cried. "Help! I'm down here!"

But there was nothing but silence. Where was everybody?

He reached an area of rocks at the edge of the lagoon

and tried to get some kind of hold on the muddy walls surrounding him, to find some kind of footing, but it was too slippery, and he fell back in the water every time. "Hey! Anyone up there? Help!" he called again.

Ominously, from the darkness, he heard a sound that was all too familiar.

Tick-tock, tick-tock.

Maybe after all this time, Harry would get his real hook at last. He found he wasn't looking forward to that possibility as much as he'd imagined.

"Get me out of here!" He scrambled against the slick mud walls, trying to use his hook for leverage, but it kept slipping off the surface. Harry was about to panic. It was dark and the lagoon was deep. He could not see the far side, so he dared not try to swim across it. He was stuck here at the rocky edge of the water, clambering for a foothold.

Tick-tock, tick-tock.

Once old Tick-Tock got a taste of him, he was sure to want more.

He fumbled over more rocks, tripped, and hit the water. He stood and tried again, feeling his way through the darkness.

Tick-tock, tick-tock.

Closer and closer.

Harry ran backward, splashing across the narrow edge of the lagoon, but the sound only got louder. It was all around him. There was no use in running. Nowhere to hide.

Nowhere to go. So he did the first thing that came to mind: Harry shut his eyes and prepared to be chomped.

A moment passed.

Tick-tock, tick-tock.

That terrible ticking persisted, but no crocodile arrived. He waited for the titanic jaws to close around his head, for the forelegs to clamp his neck, but nothing touched him. There was only darkness, the water, and the rocks.

He stepped back, and his foot touched sand. It was dry and sturdy. The hole he'd fallen in was larger than he'd realized. Out of the water, he followed a sandy beach, stumbling in the dark, hoping his head wouldn't smash into some unseen wall.

Tick-tock, tick-tock.

The sound hadn't been coming from the water: it was out on the sand somewhere. Harry had a good idea what was making it, so this time he ran toward it.

The cave opened into a wider space where a hole in the distant ceiling sent shafts of light streaming into the cavern like golden spears. They faintly illuminated a great pile of discarded objects, including an old alarm clock.

"So that's what made all that ticking," he said, though there was no one else within earshot. Now that he thought about it, the tick-tock had been a bit too loud to be the tick-tocking of the clock the old croc had swallowed.

Harry rooted through the pile, finding glass canisters

full of strange and wondrous items: NEWT'S SPLEEN read one, EAGLE EYES another. There were candlesticks and candelabras, silver snuffboxes, crystal balls, iron cauldrons, and bloodstained tarot cards. He threw each and every piece aside until at last, beneath all that junk stood a treasure chest, exactly as Sophie had described.

He grabbed it and tucked it under his arm, just as he heard his name being called.

"Harry!" Uma said, materializing in the darkness, holding a torch above her head. He almost jumped out of his boots at the sound of her voice.

"You all right?" said Uma. "We didn't know where you went. All we saw was this crumbling hole in the ground. It collapsed just after you fell through it, but we dug it out again. We tried calling to you, but you didn't answer, so we just climbed down after you."

Harry grinned. "Yeah, I'm all right. Thanks, Captain."

She smiled, and Harry realized it was the first time he'd fully acknowledged that she was captain and meant it.

Behind her was the rest of the crew, ropes coiled around their shoulders. "Ooh, what's that?" Gil said, seeing a skull in the assemblage of magical items.

"Don't touch it!" cried Uma, but it was too late.

A whirling red cloud shot out of the skull, and the pirates cowered, fearing the worst. But the red mist only turned into a butterfly and dissipated.

"Phew," said Gil.

"Don't touch anything else!" barked Uma. "Leave it all alone!"

"Look," Harry said. "I found it."

"The treasure chest!" Uma cried. "Open it."

Harry set the treasure chest on the ground gently. All of them gathered around it, Harry and Uma, Gil, and the rest of the pirates. They'd come far and risked much to find this little chest. All of them were eager to see its contents.

"Ready?" Harry asked.

"Ready," said Uma. "Show me my mother's necklace."

Harry pried the lid of the treasure chest and it opened with a great creak.

And that's when all the skeletons appeared.

chapter

29

Rivals

*B*en didn't argue against Mal's urgent assessment of the situation. Whatever it was, it had to be dire if Mal wanted them to hurry like that. "You guys go," urged Jane. "I'll keep an eye on things over here and make sure my mom doesn't meddle again."

"Thanks, Jane," said Carlos. "You saved us."

"It was the least I could do," she said, flushing pink. "Now go, run. Go do what you need to do."

Ben commandeered the royal racer, the fastest car in all of Auradon, and they all crowded into it, which was kind of a problem since it was built for two and the backseat was designed for carting either dogs or picnic baskets, and certainly not three friend-size bodies.

"You guys all right back there?" he asked, taking the wheel with Mal in the passenger seat.

"Sort of," said Evie, who had the advantage of being small and flexible, while the boys contorted themselves to fit in the space.

"Not really!" said Carlos. "Please hurry!"

"That's my neck!" said Jay, who had pretzelled himself behind the driver's seat.

Ben drove them back to the marina, and Mal filled him in as promised on the loss of the trident and the Uma situation. "Everyone on the Isle is really looking for this?"

"That's what Evie's mirror showed," said Mal. "And if anyone could find it, it's Uma. Knowing her, she won't give up until she's got it."

"Why does she want it so badly?" Ben wondered aloud.

"I don't know, probably because she thinks she can finish the job I was supposed to do, with Fairy Godmother's wand I mean. You know, get rid of the dome and free all the villains," said Mal. "She's probably even taken over my old territory by now."

"Your old territory?" asked Ben, amused. "What were you, some kind of boss lady?"

"Not some kind," interrupted Jay. "THE boss lady of the Isle."

"Shush," said Mal, a bit embarrassed about her past as

one of the most feared villains on the island. "That was before."

But Ben looked at her admiringly. "Of course you were the best lady boss. I wouldn't expect anything less."

She had to admit it had been fun, terrorizing the citizens of the Isle of the Lost, Jay and the rest of the thugs by her side. "Let's just say everyone avoided getting on my bad side," Mal said proudly, feeling just a tiny bit nostalgic about the old days.

"Or else!" said Jay, raising his fist and hitting the roof with his head. "Oof!"

When they arrived at the harbor, the royal speedboat was just as they'd left it, as if waiting for their return. Ben jumped off the deck and onto the speedboat's helm, helping Mal and Evie aboard. The boys followed right behind.

Jay bowed and motioned toward the wheel. "Your Highness," he said jokingly, but with a hint of seriousness as well.

"You can drive this thing, right?" Mal asked Ben.

Ben nodded. "I should, I've been taking lessons all my life."

"Princes," Jay said, rolling his eyes. "So many lessons."

"Archery, horseback-riding, sailing, boating, swords-and-shields, dancing, manners, etiquette, statesmanship," said Ben, counting them off in his head.

"Is there anything you can't do?" asked Carlos, curious.

"I'm sure there's a ton of things I can't do," said Ben.

"I sort of doubt it," said Carlos.

"Where are we headed?" asked Ben, as Carlos and Jay saw to pulling off the ropes that secured the boat to the dock.

"Evie?" asked Mal.

Evie pulled out her magic mirror. "Yup, it looks like the trident is still under the waters by the Isle of the Doomed, over on the far side of Goblin Beach. I can see the dome shimmering."

Ben nodded and the boat pulled out of the harbor. The waters were calm by Auradon Bay, but became rockier and harder to navigate once they reached the Strait of Ursula.

A fine mist coated the Isle of the Lost, and everyone had to hold on to the handles on the side on the boat, lest they be thrown into the water by the increasingly large waves. "Over there?" asked Ben, as they came closer and closer to the foggy mist.

"Yes! To the left!" said Carlos, yelling to be heard above the crashing waves and the distant roar of thunder.

"How are we going to slip through the barrier?" asked Evie.

"We're not going to," said Mal. "Ben, just get us as close as you can."

Ben steered toward the edge of the mist.

"I see Goblin Beach!" called Jay. "Right through there."

"Evie, how are we doing?"

Evie checked the mirror. "We're getting closer. But I'm worried someone else could get to it first."

"Hurry," urged Mal, as Ben gassed the engine and zoomed forward. The speedboat jumped through the waves.

"We'll get there just in time!" said Carlos, navigating with Jay.

Mal felt the usual excitement and adrenaline of a well-matched competition. This was just like when she used to race her toad against Uma's for all the dirty candy in Ursula's shop. Except this time, the winner didn't get toad pee all over their hands.

chapter
30

Skeleton Island

The skeletons came out of the darkness, descending from the sky like ghosts, their calcium-white bones glistening in the light of Uma's torch. They danced in the black, their limbs making herky-jerky motions up and down, bobbing as they walked.

Gil screamed and fell backward, splashing water everywhere. Uma thought one of the skeletons might have struck him with its sword. Harry bent to check for wounds, while the skeletons drifted closer, dipping up and down, their feet hardly touching the ground.

What magic was this? Uma was confused. How was

this all happening? And now there were more skeletons, descending from the dark reaches of the cavern's ceiling, a place so distant that not even her torchlight could reach it.

The crew formed ranks, drawing their swords and readying one another for the fight, but their faces were as white as the skeletons'. This was a hardened crew, but none of them had ever seen anything like this, not even Uma.

"Gil's okay," said Harry.

"Just a bit of wounded pride," said Gil as he shook the water from his hair, stumbling backward to avoid the approaching skeletons. They were all retreating, but the lagoon was at their backs, so with each step they took they were forced to walk deeper into the water. This could only go on for so long before they'd need to stop and fight.

But the skeletons didn't pass the water's edge. They hung there, waiting, their twirling swords and nodding heads tempting the pirates into battle. Uma had never been one to turn down a fight, so she rallied her crew and stormed the beach. "At my back, you cowards."

Shamed by her courage, the pirates called out battle cries and emerged from the water, splashing onto the beach.

Uma swung at the nearest skeleton with all her fury, hoping to nick a bone or perhaps to break a rib or two but instead its entire rib cage shattered, sending bones flying in all directions, landing in the water with a hundred different splashes.

Encouraged by her success, she struck the next skeleton, this one at the neck. The spinal cord popped in two, the body falling limply to the sand, but the head stayed where it was, bobbing in the air. It *had* to be some kind of magic, but she could barely make out anything besides the skull floating in the air. She struck it with her sword and it just rolled to one side, swinging back and forth like a pendulum, rocking like a child on a swing.

"It's on a rope," she said. Uma slashed at the darkness above the skull, severing the cord, sending the head tumbling onto the beach. A quick inspection revealed a whole series of thin black ropes that were tethered all over the skeletons. Some mechanism must have been jerking them up and down, back and forth, like marionettes on a string.

"They're not alive!" Uma said. "It's not magic! It's just a trick! Keep moving!"

"There must be some machine up there, embedded in the cavern's ceiling," she said. The black strings were nearly invisible in the dark cave.

Harry nodded. He was going over the fallen skeleton, inspecting the ropes, some of which were still connected to the machine. A severed hand leaped upward from the beach, dangling in his face, sword still in its grasp. Harry slashed at the cord and the arm fell limply to the sand, but the whole thing was unnerving.

By now, the rest of the pirates were all slashing at the ropes. But they could only cut so many, so the dead continued their dance. Pieces of broken arms and legs kept jerking about in the air.

"I never thought they were alive," said Harry, as he pushed against a skeleton, sending it swinging away. But it swung right back, hitting him so hard it knocked him to the ground.

"Maybe they don't need to be alive to take you down," Uma joked.

Even if these were mechanical skeletons, their blades were real enough that they could still do damage.

"Be careful," she cautioned her crew. "Cut the ropes, watch out for the swords, and someone fetch me that torch. We need light!"

One of the crewmen retrieved the still-flaming torch that Uma had dropped near the water's edge. He held it high above them all, revealing at last an elaborate web of strings and cables, all of them disappearing upward toward the cavern's ceiling.

In spite of their increased illumination, Harry got his hook wrapped up in a skeleton hand. He twisted to and fro before finally getting so caught in the cables he fell to the sand. Gil was doing a little better, having wrestled one of the skeletons to the ground and stomped all over its bones. He slashed the ropes when he was finished. The rest of the crew howled their battle cries, as they took down the cables.

Uma growled, annoyed that it was taking them so long

to escape. It was a booby trap. Which meant there were others.

"Keep cutting strings!" she ordered. "And try to do it with a bit more organization."

Taking her advice, the pirates went about cutting the ropes in a more coordinated manner, moving down the line, slashing just above the heads so the skeletons would fall limply to the beach in a single cut. One after another they dropped to the sand, a great pile of bones and cords forming at their feet.

As the last skeleton fell to the ground at last, a low thrum echoed in the darkness.

"What was that?" she cried, as an arrow struck the stone next to her. An inch to the right and it would have split her head in two.

The soft whistle of bowstrings reverberated in the darkness. All the pirates had hit the sand after seeing the first arrow, flattening themselves as best they could as the barrage sailed over their heads.

"When we cut that last skeleton it must have triggered some new part of the mechanism," said Harry.

"I guessed as much," said Uma. The real question was, what was coming next? It was clear the sorcerer had no intention of letting anyone take what was in that treasure chest. Some of the pirates had already stood, but Uma heard a distant clicking—and a winding sound.

"Duck!" said Uma, and the pirates slammed once more onto the sand, covering themselves with their hands, or whatever else they could use for shields, from a new assault of arrows.

"The machine rewound itself," said Uma. "It paused after the first volley, just to trick anyone who was clever enough to avoid the first, before it sent out another attack."

"So what do we do now?" asked Gil. "I can't stay here with my face pressed in the muck." Indeed the boy's knees were sunk in the water, and his face was dabbed with mud. Most of the pirates weren't in much better shape. All of them were wet. And only half had made it fully out of the water before they'd had to drop.

"Listen," said Uma.

"To what?" asked Harry.

"To the silence. The machine stopped." She motioned for everyone to stand. One by one they lifted themselves from the muck, their feet making terrible slurping sounds. They were wet and dirty but alive.

Uma took a deep breath. The machine had stopped, but she doubted they were out of danger yet. "Come on!" she said, leading them toward a narrow finger of light in the distance, indicating a way out of the cave.

She took a step toward it, and felt something tense and release beneath her foot as the earth shifted. From a distance, she heard an ominous rumbling.

"I think I triggered something," said Uma. "The machine's going again."

Dust sifted downward from the ceiling, followed by a low thunder that nearly shook her to her knees. Rocks fell from the cavern ceiling, and they could hear stones breaking all around them.

"The cavern's collapsing!" Uma cried, but by then they'd all figured it out. This must be the final trap, the one that would seal them in the cave with the treasure chest forever.

The sorcerer had obviously been serious about the safety of these formerly magical objects. Even without magic at his disposal, he had successfully created obstacles that would deter even the hardiest and greediest goblin.

But Uma was no goblin, and she was determined to leave the Isle of the Doomed with the only inheritance she would ever receive from her mother's past.

"Run!" she called.

"Already there!" said Harry, at her side, Gil puffing not far behind.

Uma waved her cutlass in the air. "Follow me!" she said, leading the crew toward the light. All around them, stones pelted their heads. The air was already filled with dust, but a light shone faintly in the distance so they ran toward it. The very earth beneath their feet was collapsing as they went, and the walls were falling behind them.

Uma was the first to make it to the cave's mouth, but she stayed there, waiting for each member of her crew to pass. The captain was always the last to leave, after all, the one who went down with her ship. She would not budge until the last pirate was out. Luckily the pirates were a frightened bunch, so they ran like children, tumbling over one another to get out of the cave as quickly as possible. Uma stepped out of the cavern just as the last stone broke, and the ceiling collapsed entirely, forever trapping whatever was left in there.

"We made it," he muttered, stating the obvious, as she stumbled out onto the sand, her hair caked with dust and tiny stones. Harry brushed a rock off her shoulder.

In a panic, she looked around. All she saw were pirates, shaking the mud from their hair and brushing it from their clothes. "Where is it? The treasure chest?" she demanded. In all the confusion—in their sheer desire to get out of there—had they left the one thing they had come to find?

Harry tapped her on the shoulder.

What did he want? He didn't have it either!

But he reached underneath his arm and revealed what he had been carrying the entire time. The treasure chest.

Without hesitating Uma flipped open its wooden lid. There was an old yellowed envelope inside. Uma pulled it out.

"'Ursula,'" she read, examining the spiky handwriting on the envelope.

Then she shook out the contents onto her palm. There it was, her mother's seashell necklace, except it was in a hundred tiny little pieces. "I forgot it was broken."

"Nothing a little island sludge can't put back together," said Harry. "Come on. We've got a bucket of the stuff back on the ship. It's stronger than glue; it'll work."

chapter
31

Pirate's Booty

itting each of the pieces of the broken seashell together was like trying to put together a puzzle without any reference as to what it should look like. They knew it was a shell, but they had no idea where this ridge or that one should fit. It took patience and attention to detail, and they'd just fought a band of skeletons, dodged arrows, and escaped a disintegrating cave. No one was in the mood for a bit of jewelry repair. But there was no time to waste, so they set themselves about the task—clearing a great table and making certain it was clean before Uma placed the envelope's contents upon it.

"How do we know we even have all the pieces to this thing?" said Uma, frustrated.

"We don't," agreed Harry. "But if we give up now, we'll never find out."

"Shush," said Gil, who was placing each piece back together with a delicacy the others hadn't known he was capable of. They had to trace the edges of each piece, looking for ridges and bumps that matched another piece or a streak of color that ran from one fragment to the next. It was subtle work, almost impossible. Harry threw up his hands more than once, and Uma twice had to take a walk out on the deck to let loose a bit of frustration. They all took turns at the task, but it was Gil, oddly enough, who stuck with it, supervising the whole thing. The work was painstaking, until Gil finally made an announcement. "Okay," he said, "we're missing one piece."

"Honestly?" muttered Uma.

"It might have fallen under the table," said Harry. "Everyone look!" He stood and knelt on the floor to see if he could find a tiny gold piece. Gil, Uma, and the rest of the crew did the same. They looked everywhere and even sent some of the crew back to the beach to see if one of the pieces had fallen out when Uma first opened the envelope. They found nothing.

Perhaps it was lost in the sea, thought Uma.

She recalled her mother telling her about that final

battle. How Ursula had called the great waves, urging them to skyscraper-like heights, and how she had blown up to a thousand times her size—a large, laughing octopus, larger than the ship, loud as thunder. How she had cursed them all, wreaking havoc on Prince Eric's ship, and aiming to drown all aboard.

Except Prince Eric had taken the wheel and rammed his ship right into her heart, right into her necklace, scattering its pieces all over the ocean. Uma always held her breath at that part of the story, wondering how it was that her mother had survived such a battle. Because even though she'd lost, she'd survived. Prince Eric hadn't destroyed her completely.

And here was the necklace.

Here was hope.

A way out of this island prison.

A way out of stagnation and broken dreams, endless routine, and a future that went nowhere.

Harry was shaking his head. He slammed his fist against the nearest table, sending the plates and cups jumping. "It's not here."

He'd given up, and Uma felt the same pain run through her. It just wasn't fair, to come this close only to be missing one miniscule little piece.

Uma took the seashell in hand and looked at it carefully. "Maybe we don't need the missing piece," she said. It was a chip barely larger than a hairline crack. That was all.

"I don't know," said Harry. "It looks incomplete."

"What about your locket?" asked Gil. "Didn't you say there was something in there?"

Uma gasped. She'd almost forgotten about the locket she always wore. What had her mother said when she'd given it to her? *It's all I have left.* All Ursula had left of what? They were about to find out. Uma swung the chain over her head and held it out so everyone could see it. Then she carefully pried open the top with her fingernail. It flipped up with a snap, revealing a sliver of gold.

"That's it!" said Harry.

"I think it just might be the last piece," said Uma. It looked to be the right shape, but she wouldn't be sure until they'd fit it into place. Her heart skipped a beat as she lowered it into the opening.

It fit perfectly. "Gil, sludge me."

Gil handed her the bucket of sludge, and they all watched, holding their breath, as Uma glued the final piece onto the shell. She could have sworn there was even a flash of light, but maybe it was just the gold reflecting off the moonlight through the window.

It was done. The shell was complete.

"There," Uma said with satisfaction. "I think that's it." She studied her handiwork. The shell glittered in her palm— history, legacy, and tragedy in each curve of its shape. She held it up for everyone to see. "Ursula's necklace!" she cried.

"Put it on," said Harry.

She nodded, undid the clasp, and draped the necklace over her collarbone. The gold was warm against her skin, and she felt a faint echo of its former power. It had the sense and shape of her mother's wrath. One of the greatest treasures of the sea, and it was in her hands.

"All right?" said Harry.

Uma nodded. "I can feel it," she said, holding the gold seashell between her pointer finger and thumb. "It's almost like it's alive."

"Excellent," said Harry. "Where to, Captain?" he asked, a hand on the wheel.

Uma whispered to the seashell, "Find me the trident."

She felt the shell tilt slightly to the right, like a compass, just as Cook told her it would. The necklace and the trident, as the most powerful objects from the underwater kingdom, were linked. Drawn to each other like magnets.

"West," she said. "It's due west of us."

"West it is. To the trident!" cried Harry. "Avast, me hearties! Flip up the jib! Haul anchor! Let's go!" he ordered, rushing around.

"To the trident!" cried Gil. "Um, what's a trident?" he asked.

Uma took the scope and looked through the lens. In the distance, she could see Auradon, the mainland. *Soon*, she thought. Soon she would have Triton's trident, and she and her crew would be off this cursed island forever.

Showdown

Now I am the ruler
of all the ocean!
The waves obey my
every whim!
The sea and its spoils
bow down to my power!
—Ursula,
The Little Mermaid

chapter

32

Into the Deep

*U*ma scanned the horizon. Countless waves dotted the sea, crashing higher and higher, curling into whitecaps, the wind catching the water and throwing it into the air. The sky was dark with clouds, but even so, she thought she saw something in the distance, headed toward them from the opposite side of the bay—the Auradon side. She thought it might be driftwood at first, but it was moving quickly against the wind. "Do you see something over there?" she asked, focusing on a small dot that she could barely make out through the wind and fog.

Harry picked up a telescope. "Yeah, I see it. It's on the other side of the barrier, and it's heading toward us."

Uma gnashed her teeth, annoyed at this unexpected arrival from an unknown party. "What does it look like?"

"I don't know. We'll need to get closer, but it must be some sort of boat," said Harry.

"They're moving against the wind, which means they've got a powerful speedboat of some kind," said Uma.

"But why are they here and why now? Fishing? No one ever comes this close to the Isle of the Lost. All the Auradon folks like to stay on their side of the channel," said Harry. "They know what's good for them."

"I don't think they're out here to fish," said Uma. "It's not exactly fishing weather." The waves were taller now, and each time they struck them, the ship was cast upward, then quickly set down again, loudly thumping into the gap between the waves before the next one hit and sprayed the deck with water. All in all, it was miserable progress, but at least they were moving quickly. Just not quickly enough for comfort. Uma took to the telescope to monitor the progress of the boat they'd spotted. She had a bad feeling about this.

Worse, it began to pour. The skies cracked with thunder and all around them the air darkened as raindrops pelted the ship.

"Harry! Can't you make us go faster?" she ordered. The

necklace kept tugging toward the right, and it appeared the trident was somewhere close by. But Goblin Beach was almost endlessly long.

"Aye, aye, Captain," said Harry. "I believe we've done all we can, short of throwing over any excess cargo. A light ship is a fast ship, if either of you would care to jump over the side? Or maybe I can make the wind blow a bit harder?"

"Well, if anyone can do it, you can," said Uma.

"I'm on it," said Harry, raising his chin and mockingly blowing toward the sails. "There," he said. "Now I've done everything."

Uma balled her fists in annoyance. In truth, she knew Harry had done everything possible to get them moving as quickly as their sails would allow. They were cruising at a considerable clip to the other side of the island, but so was the other ship—and there was no doubt now that they were both headed to the same place. Plus she didn't need the tele-scope to know it was moving faster than they were.

"It's below there," said Uma, as the necklace in her hand began to heat up. "I can feel it. We're at the right place. Can you get us closer?"

Harry squinted, measuring the distance. "Too many rocks for this big a ship, and with all the sails unfurled we're moving too fast to navigate those waters. We'll have to anchor and take out the rowboat."

He stowed the sails as quickly as possible, while Gil

tossed out the anchor. They had to fiddle with it a bit, waiting until the great hook caught hold of the sea bottom. The rope snapped tight, and they were moored.

Harry indicated a small boat with only a pair of paddles. "That's our ride, if you want your trident. It's the only way into those rocks," he said.

It didn't look promising, but it was all they had, so Uma, Harry, and Gil clambered into the rickety boat, and Harry and Gil rowed Uma closer to the edge of the beach. The rocks made it difficult to navigate, and since both of the boys were facing the wrong direction, they had to rely on Uma to tell them which way to go.

"Right!" she exclaimed, but the boat went left. "My right, you idiots," she said, correcting them. "Left now, just a bit. Now right again." Uma had to stand at the bow and push off the rocks to keep from colliding with them. It was a veritable maze and they were forced to go this way and that, back and forth. At points the rocks were so dense they had to stop paddling altogether. All Harry and Gil could do then was push off manually against the stones.

"Come on, faster," said Uma. "This is taking too long."

"You're welcome to get out and pull us," huffed Harry, straining with exertion.

Uma frowned, but she got up and pushed against the rocks as well until they were clear, finding themselves in a circle of clear blue water not far from the beach. She stood and glanced down into the depths, spotting something gold glinting through the seaweed.

King Triton's trident!

Her heart leaped with wicked glee. "This is it!" she said, readying to dive down and take it.

The trident was hers!

chapter

33

Power and Glory

The Isle of the Doomed loomed larger and larger through the mist as they got closer to their destination. Mal had forgotten how foreboding the mysterious island looked, especially with Maleficent's fortress built right on the top of the tallest cliff, casting gloomy shadows everywhere.

"Hurry!" said Mal urgently, as Evie checked her mirror.

Jay scanned through the fog, just as it began to rain. "Look!" he yelled, as a huge pirate ship came into view on the other side of the beachhead.

"Uma!" cried Evie. "She's already here!"

"Ben! Faster!" urged Mal.

"I'm trying," said Ben. But it was hard to navigate the three-foot-tall waves, and all of them were drenched.

"Turn left again!" said Carlos, tracking the trident's possible location on the map and attempting to navigate the rough waters.

Ben steered the boat left, and they all leaned forward and tried not to fall off.

"Uma's found it!" yelled Evie, as she watched Uma stand up from the little rowboat. "She's diving for it!"

"No!" cried Mal. "She can't have it! Ben, come on!"

Ben zoomed the boat over to an inlet by the Isle of the Doomed. They couldn't see anything in all the fog and rain, and as he turned the boat, it crashed against the barrier. "This is as close as I can get us," he said, trying to keep his eyes open against the howling wind and rain.

"Mal, do it now!" said Carlos.

"Jay, take the wheel," said Ben, as he jumped to the boat's hood, balancing himself as it was rocked by the waves. He offered a hand to Mal. "Come on!"

Mal climbed up from the dashboard next to Ben, holding her spell book tightly. Waves lashed against the boat, and it was hard to stand upright. She stumbled, but Ben caught her. "I've got you," he said, his hands steady against her waist.

She shot him a quick smile and opened the book to the spell she needed. A simple one—even a child could use it. *"Spark and fire, elf and gnome, open up this invisible dome!*" she cried. For a moment nothing happened; then a small, pinprick-size hole appeared in the invisible barrier. It grew larger and larger until Mal was able to thrust her arm through the unseen wall.

"It worked!" she said, laughing in relief.

"Get the trident!" yelled Ben.

"Too late!" cried Evie, watching the mirror. "Uma's got it!"

Mal wanted to curse, until she realized creating a hole in the dome meant that she could use a little magic within the barrier for a change. And a little magic was all she needed. She checked her watch; it was not yet fifteen after the top of the hour.

"*Time and tide, wind and night! Turn the clock back to the top!*" she chanted, and time went backward for everyone else just enough to give Mal time to grab the trident before Uma could lay her hands on it.

"Whoa, what just happened," said Carlos, confused.

"Mal turned the time back; it's okay, you'll get used to it," said Evie. "Mal, now! Uma's back on her boat, she doesn't have the trident yet!"

Mal opened her palm. She'd written the spell on her own, and hoped it would work. "*Demon heart and all things abhorrent, bring me the sea king's missing trident!*"

But no trident appeared, only more sheets of rain.

What was going on?

It turned out a little bit of magic was all her opponent

needed as well, and with the hole in the barrier still open, Uma was tapping into a power of her own. She stood on the rowboat and held a golden seashell necklace, which glowed in the darkness.

"Uma's using Ursula's necklace—it's pulling on the trident too!" said Evie, watching the mirror intently.

Mal's spell and Uma's necklace each drew the trident, causing a magnetic force that roiled the seas, angering and confusing the waves. The wind lashed with fury, and rain stormed on the water.

Mal wiped her hair from her eyes. She was soaking wet and shivering in her leather jacket. Lightning struck the skies, thunder rolled, and the waves got bigger and bigger, threatening to overpower the speedboat. They wouldn't last out here much longer. She had to get that trident away from Uma.

Evie was almost thrown overboard, but Carlos caught her hand in time. "One hand for you, and one hand for the ship," he advised, as the skies cracked open overhead once again.

"Bring me King Triton's trident!" Mal called, her arm straining across the barrier. She felt the power of the spell through her body as she bent her will toward recovering that trident from the ocean floor.

From afar, she could see the golden trident as it wavered in its rise toward her enemy. It stalled, floating in the ocean, then slowly began to wrench toward her.

"It's working!" yelled Evie.

The energy around their boat crackled as the necklace and the spell fought for supremacy over the trident and the trident moved toward the speedboat.

"To me!" Mal cried, using every last ounce of her will and magic to bring it forward.

It jerked toward their boat, just a hairbreadth away.

But at the very last second, the trident twisted around, moving closer to the Isle of the Lost, closer to Uma.

chapter
34

Evil Enchantment

Magic! What was this? There was magic in the air. It crackled with furious energy. Uma could feel it emanating from the seashell necklace and pervading the very atmosphere around her. She had no idea why it was there, or how it happened, or why she had a strange, vague memory of swimming down to the bottom of the sea and actually placing her hands on the trident, but she could feel magic all around her and she knew exactly what to do.

Uma held up her mother's necklace. "Bring me Triton's greatest treasure!" she called, and she held up the necklace a bit higher. For a moment, she felt the wind swirl, picking up the necklace and twirling it around her fingers. The sky darkened to a deeper shade of gray and the boat pitched back and forth. Water splashed the deck.

There was a loud *boom* as thunder rolled. Lightning lit the sky with streaks of white and blue. A cool wind swept the boat, and Uma felt the presence of something otherworldly. The necklace and the trident called to each other. She felt the pull; it was all around her.

The very air vibrated with power, and the seashell became hot in her hand, glowing fiery through her clenched fist. Light emanated from the shell, turning her face a pale shade of orange, making her fingers glow. The wind blew her hair off her shoulders.

"What's happening?" said Gil, as the orange glow of the seashell grew brighter and the power Uma sought drew nearer. Soon all of them were lit in shades of red and orange. The light pulsated, washing over them in waves.

"I can feel it!" Uma called. "It's coming up!"

A vortex formed in the water, a churning, swirling funnel, and there was something at the bottom of it.

Harry peered over the side of the boat into the dark depths. "There!" he cried.

Uma looked down, and she could almost see it, the tip of the trident emerging from the bottom of the vortex. There it was, twinkling gold . . . just out of her reach. . . .

Closer . . .

Closer . . .

Closer . . .

The trident was rising now, flying out of the water. It was nearly within their grasp. The wind howled, and the rain poured down. The water spun in a furious circle, threatening to draw them down into it, just as the trident came near. The boys whooped in victory. Against the wind and the current, they paddled toward the trident, but the boat pitched violently, side to side, dipping and leaning as the wind and waves cast them to and fro.

"Grab it!" cried Harry. "I can't keep this up much longer. In a minute, we'll capsize, and then we'll be swimming."

"Or sucked down into that vortex," said Gil.

Uma ignored their pessimism. The trident was all she cared about. The shell glowed wildly; the trident rose. They were close now, terribly close—but as Harry warned, they were just as close to falling into the water as they were to catching hold of the trident. Uma wouldn't celebrate until that golden staff was safely on board. None of them would.

"Do it!" Harry cried again. This time they were finally at the trident. They rowed as near as they dared, fighting the current, trying to stay upright as the wind whirled and the water twisted around the mighty golden spear.

"This is it," said Harry.

"We're close enough," said Uma. Through the dark fog she could make out the shape of a speedboat on the other side of the barrier. She was sure its occupants had come for the trident too, but they were too late.

Uma had reached it first.

There it was, rising, like a phoenix from the ashes. Triton's greatest treasure. It would be hers!

She reached out—it was only a few more feet away . . . inches . . . All she had to do was grasp it. . . .

chapter
35

All for One

al felt the prize slipping away from her, but
at the very last second, she chanted the spell
again, forcing her immense will on the trident. Suddenly, it
hurtled toward her like a missile.

Mal gasped as the trident slammed into her palm, and
she clenched her fist around it. It jerked and twisted in her
grasp, and Mal could see powerful energy waves around it,
attempting to pull it in the opposite direction. Mal tried to
hold it with both hands, but the energy from Uma's necklace
pulled off her left glove, sending it soaring away.

Mal yanked the trident through the hole in the barrier.
"I've got it!"

"The barrier!" Carlos reminded her.

"Elf and gnome, close this dome!" she yelled, and the hole in the invisible barrier shut with a snap. The magnetic energy around the trident immediately disappeared, and her hand dropped suddenly as the tension vanished. The shock of it sent her flying into Evie, who fell overboard.

Mal clutched the trident and crouched on top of the boat, searching the churning ocean. "EVIE!" she screamed. "EVIE, NO!"

Jay steered the boat around the waves as they frantically searched for their friend.

"EVIE!" called Jay.

"Evie, come on!" yelled Carlos.

Come back to me, Mal thought fiercely, hanging on to the edge of the railing. *Come back, Evie.* She wished so hard, she thought her head would explode; still there was nothing but the raging sea and the crash of thunder and lightning.

"You guys," said Jay. "The storm is just getting stronger. We're going to sink."

"I think I saw her over there!" yelped Ben. "Circle around!"

"EVIE!" Mal cried. "Where are you?"

But still there was nothing. The largest wave they'd ever seen rose from the ocean and slammed hard onto the boat, throwing them against each other.

"I can't keep us afloat much longer!" Jay cried.

Just when it seemed they were going to capsize, Evie

emerged from the water, her arms flailing. Mal was spent from using her magic, and fell limply against the railing. "Help her! I don't know what to do," she cried, keeping a tight grip on the trident.

But her friends picked up the slack, moving with precise urgency. "We're too far away for her to swim," said Ben. "Quick, Carlos, grab a life ring. Jay, you have the best arm, throw it to her!"

Ben took the wheel of the speedboat while Jay tossed the orange floatie as far as he could. "EVIE! GRAB IT!"

Evie caught the ring with one hand and held on, keeping her head above the waves.

"PULL!" yelled Ben, steering the boat as Jay and Carlos tugged mightily on the rope, bringing Evie back despite the waves and the rain, inch by inch, until at last she was floating by their side.

"Evie! I thought we'd lost you!" Mal cried joyfully, tears of relief falling down her cheeks and mingling with the rain as she leaned over to help Carlos and Jay haul her back onto the boat. "Are you okay?"

"You're okay, you're okay," said Carlos, smacking Evie's back to help her cough up seawater.

"Here," said Jay, handing Evie a warm towel he'd run to grab from belowdecks and helping Carlos drape it over her shoulders.

Evie leaned on Mal, still shaky on her feet. "I'm okay, thanks to you guys."

Mal gave Evie a tight hug. "I don't know what I would do without you! Don't ever scare me like that again!"

"You scared all of us," said Ben, letting Jay steer the boat once more. "That was intense. But you got it, Mal?"

"I got it," she said, handing him the trident.

"We did it," Ben said.

"We did it," she said, not quite believing it, as Ben held the golden trident in his hands.

"We did it together." He nodded. Then he turned to Jay, who was back at the wheel. "Come on, let's get out of here before we sink."

chapter
36

Lost Revenge

"Where did it go?" yelled Uma, as the trident disappeared right before her eyes, and she was thrown backward onto the rowboat, falling hard on her back. Her hat tumbled off her head, and she scrambled to catch it before recovering her balance. "Where's the trident?" she screamed, looking for it on the floor of the boat, even though she knew it was gone.

Lightning flashed overhead, and waves crashed against the boat, dumping water all over them. The necklace's chain had snapped, and she almost lost hold of it. The rain was relentless, and the whirlwind doubled its speed, spinning them around in a dizzying spiral, obscuring their vision.

"Do you have it!" cried Harry. "Uma! Where's the trident?!"

Uma scanned the waters frantically but saw nothing. "It was mine!" she howled. "I almost had it! It was right there!"

"Where?" yelled Harry. "I don't see anything!"

"I don't know!" she yelled back.

"Do you have it or not?" screamed Harry, as six-foot waves roared and crashed over the little dinghy. He had to fight to hold on to the oars and steer the boat back to the *Lost Revenge*.

But Uma was too dazed to answer; she was still trying to get back up and resume her balance.

"Gil!" Harry cried, just as the boat lurched upward and slammed back down, throwing Gil overboard.

"Where's Gil?" yelled Uma, trying to be heard above the whistle of the wind.

"I don't know! He fell over!" cried Harry, as he lunged to grab an oar that had slipped from its hold, before it could be lost to the sea as well.

Without hesitation, Uma jumped off the boat and into the churning water to save Gil.

Harry saw a brown hat bobbing up and down in the froth. "He's over there!"

"Help!" screamed Gil, scrambling in the waves. "Help!"

Gil went under, and Harry feared the worst—but suddenly, Uma's turquoise head appeared by his side. Slowly but surely, she swam them back to safety.

When they reached the dinghy, Harry leaned over and hauled them both back aboard. Gil coughed and choked and spewed water all over the deck.

"Ew," said Uma. "You're welcome."

That was too close. They needed to get back to the ship if they were going to survive, so she motioned for the boys to start rowing. Fighting against the thundering waves, the pouring rain, and the howling winds, they finally reached the *Lost Revenge*, where the other pirates threw a rope ladder down the side.

"Captains first," Harry said, giving a hand to help Uma climb the rope.

Uma nodded and hoisted herself up. Gil went up next, and Harry last.

The crew was vainly trying to keep the ship upright as it lurched wildly from side to side, at the mercy of the roiling, angry sea. Uma, Harry, and Gil ran to the decks, helping to hold the sail, while trying to stay away from the boom—which was swinging wildly with the wind—as well as all three masts, which were threatening to break and splinter. The storm raged around them, pouring rain all over everyone and everything.

"Let's get out of here!" yelled Harry. "We need to go back! The storm's too strong!" He took the wheel of the ship and brought it around, making for the Isle of the Lost.

But as the *Lost Revenge* reached its destination, the waves pounded against the hull, finally sending the mast crashing onto the deck, and the sails tore as it slammed right against the dock, tearing up the deck plank by plank.

Shipwrecked.

When the storm had passed, and the ship was still, the pirates groaned and assessed the wreckage. It was clear to Harry that the *Lost Revenge* would never sail again. The damage to the hull was too great.

A fine, light rain continued to fall, adding to the gloom.

Harry sighed and removed his black tricorn hat to squeeze the water from it. But he was too exhausted to be angry, and too relieved to still be alive to feel disappointment.

He looked up to see Uma standing in front of him, a confused and shocked look on her face. "I had it. I saw it, Harry. It was right there. I almost held it in my hands. The necklace worked, and there was this huge surge of magic for a moment—almost as if something had opened a hole in the dome."

"So what happened?" asked Harry.

"There was someone else there, some kind of magic," she said. "That's the only explanation."

"You're holding something," said Harry. "In your hand."

"I am?" said Uma, wonderingly. She looked down, surprised to find that Harry was right. She was holding on to something she hadn't noticed in all the commotion.

"Yeah, what've you got?" asked Gil.

Uma looked stunned to find she was holding a purple

fingerless glove with a dragon symbol embroidered on the kidskin. It could only belong to one person.

"MAL!" Uma raged, when she realized it had been none other than her fiercest rival who had been on that speedboat.

Harry had no idea why or how Mal was there at the same time they were, but there was no denying it. Mal had Triton's golden trident now, and Uma had nothing but a purple glove.

"MAL! You don't always get to win!" Uma screamed in fury.

"I think she just did," said Gil. "Didn't she?"

"Shut up, Gil," said Harry, sighing as he put his black tricorn hat back on his head.

chapter
37

No Place Like It

It was almost dawn when they returned to Auradon Prep, and Mal thought she'd never seen a sight more beautiful than the gray stone towers of the school turning pink in the sunrise. No matter that Auradon still didn't feel one hundred percent like home, she *was* home in Ben's arms. "Thanks for being there for me," she whispered.

"Always," he said, nuzzling her hair.

He gave her one more hug, then went to help the boys dock the boat in the harbor as they pulled into the bay. Evie went over to where Mal was seated and leaned her head on her friend's shoulder. "Thanks for being there for me," she said, echoing what Mal had said to Ben just moments before.

Mal leaned her purple head against Evie's and told her what Ben had said in return: "Always."

"That was close," said Jay, as he helped them climb out of the boat. "I didn't think we would make it."

"But we did," said Mal.

Jay flashed her a rueful smile. "You know it," he said, giving Ben a fist bump.

"Um, guys? I think we want this, right?" said Carlos, who'd gone to fetch the trident they'd left in the back of the boat.

Ben asked Arabella to meet them at his office, and the little mermaid practically burst into tears when she saw the trident leaning innocuously against a bookshelf.

"You did it!" she said to Ben, obviously not quite believing it was true. "You got it back!"

"We all did," said Ben with a smile, offering his hand to Mal.

Mal took it and offered her hand to Evie, who linked hands with Carlos, who took Jay's hand too. "Ben's right, we all played a part," she said. "I couldn't have done it without any of these guys."

Arabella thanked them profusely. "I'll make sure it gets back to Grandfather and the museum right away."

Ben turned to her with a serious look on his face. "Arabella, I hope you already know what I'm about to say to you."

She blushed as red as her hair. "I know, King Ben. I know. I'll never steal anything again, I promise. Fairy Godmother's right, magic is too dangerous to use." Humbled, she curtsied to Ben and left, holding the trident tightly in her hands.

"Arabella will be okay," said Mal. "I don't think she'll ever get near that trident again."

"Speaking of the museum. You guys do know that all magical artifacts belong there for safekeeping," Ben said with an embarrassed cough.

"You mean even my magic mirror?" said Evie, looking worried.

"And my spell book?" said Mal. The two girls looked askance at each other.

"I guess we should hand them over," said Evie reluctantly. "I do keep reminding Mal that we're not supposed to depend on magic." She removed the mirror from her purse and handed it to Ben.

"I'll make sure the curators get this and keep it somewhere safe," he promised. He turned to Mal expectantly.

Mal shrugged. "I left my spell book in my room," she told him. "But don't worry, I'll make sure it gets to the museum."

"Great," said Ben. "I don't know about you guys, but I think I'm going to sleep for the entire day."

"We'll get out of here," said Mal, and Ben hugged each one of them as they left, holding Mal extra tightly. She closed the door behind her with a smile.

When they were walking down the hallway, Evie nudged Mal. "He's a good king," said Evie.

"The best," said Carlos.

"You know it," said Jay.

"Yeah, I think I'll keep him around," said Mal. She and Evie said good night to the boys and headed over to the girls' dormitory.

Mal sat on the edge of her bed, chewing her thumbnail. "What's wrong?" asked Evie.

Mal sighed. She was glad Auradon was safe once more, and that they had defeated Uma, but she was still embarrassed about almost getting all of them kicked out of school and sent back to the Isle of the Lost. She'd seen the horror and fear in her friends' eyes, and while she might still feel the tug of home, she knew they felt otherwise—especially Evie, who loved Auradon. She also had to take her position as Ben's girlfriend more seriously. What she did reflected on him, on his reputation, and on his ability to govern the kingdom.

She wasn't the girl from the Isle anymore. She wasn't

just Maleficent's daughter, tagging King Beast's posters with spray paint and generally kicking up a ruckus. But she wasn't an Auradon princess either, who knew exactly how to act at every royal occasion.

If she wasn't Mal from the Isle anymore, who was she?

Later that afternoon, Mal grabbed Maleficent's spell book from her locker. She intended to walk it over to the Museum of Cultural History at some point before classes started the next day. She flipped through its well-worn pages, softly caressing each spell.

It was one of the only things she had left of her mother's, and she was loath to part with it. There was so much knowledge and wisdom in its pages. The time-turning spell had helped them retrieve the trident after all. Plus there were so many more that she loved to use. Hair spells, which had proven popular with the female segment of Auradon Prep, love spells, and anti-love spells. There were spells that brought luck or great fortune, and even a few that could turn a girl from the Isle into an Auradon princess, or a close facsimile of one. Spells for every aspect of life, truly. And while Mal understood why it had to go to the museum, that didn't mean she wanted to surrender it.

Still, she had promised Ben, and if Evie, who cherished her magic mirror as much as Mal treasured her spell book, could voluntarily give that up, then she could give up her book. Mal tucked it under her arm, determined to head to the museum before she changed her mind.

But as she walked across campus, Mal realized that while she still wasn't sure exactly who she was, she did want to make Ben happy and explore the kingdom by his side—even if the idea of all the royal events coming up made her feel just a little ill. She turned on her heel and ran all the way to her room.

"E?" she said, bursting through the door and glad to find Evie at her sewing machine as usual.

"Yes, M?" asked Evie, looking up from her task.

"I think I need some help," she said. "I've got a king-dom to meet." She counted herself lucky to have Auradon's most promising young fashion designer as her best friend and roommate. Mal decided she wanted to make a splash, and not the watery kind that left her looking like yesterday's yams.

"Do you think you could make me look more like them?" Mal asked, motioning to the wall of princesses on Evie's pin board. She wanted to look as smart as Belle, as beautiful as Cinderella, even as sweet as Aurora—but she wanted to maintain something of herself as well.

"Ooh! Yes!" said Evie, clapping her hands. "I have so many ideas. Plus, I want to show you this fabulous dress I made you for Cotillion."

"Great!" said Mal, picking up a thick fashion magazine and riffling through the pages. "When's Cotillion?"

"Oh!" said Evie. "Ben hasn't asked you yet?"

"Asked me what?" said Mal.

Evie smiled mysteriously. "You'll see."

chapter

38

Something There That Wasn't There Before

Over at his homeroom, Carlos leaned back in his seat, his exams arranged on his desk. All of them boasted A-pluses, as well as effusive praise from his teachers in the margins. *Brilliant!*—Professor Merryweather. *Astounding*—Genie. Even crotchety old Grumpy, who was teaching a seminar on Cooperation, had drawn a happy face on Carlos's paper.

Carlos smiled in satisfaction at a job well done. He was looking forward to the next semester. There were so many new elective classes to take: Language of the Stars, Enchanted Oceanography, and the Politics of the Palace, just to name a few. After having the usual fight with the registrar over his need to take over the maximum amount of classes allowed for the term, he bumped into Jane, who was wearing a brand-new blue-and-gold Auradon cheer uniform.

"You did it!" he said. "You made the team! That's awesome! Congratulations!"

"I did! Thanks so much!" Jane said, a huge smile on her face.

"What did I do?" asked Carlos.

Jane punched him in the shoulder. "You're the one who said I should try out and not give up!"

"Aw, shucks. Anyone would have told you the same thing," he said, looking down and shuffling his feet as his ears turned pink.

"But you did," said Jane. "So thank you. Are you heading that way?" she asked. "I have to meet Ben in a few minutes."

Carlos, who had been heading in the exact opposite direction, said "Yes," just so he could walk with her a little more.

"So everything worked out okay?" asked Jane. "With that secret mission?"

Carlos nodded. "Yeah, it did." He wished he could tell her all the details, but he knew it was safer for everyone if only the five of them plus Arabella knew what had happened. "It all worked out okay."

"Good." Jane looked up from behind her bangs and

smiled at him, and Carlos felt something in his heart that hadn't been there before. Something more than friendship. He couldn't stop smiling; his cheeks started to hurt.

But before he could say anything about it, Audrey ran up to them. The bossy princess looked harried. She was carrying a huge cardboard box in her arms. "Jane! Just the person I've been looking for!" she declared.

"Oh, hey, Audrey," said Jane.

"I'm so glad I found you. I need a lot of help," said Audrey.

"What's up?" asked Carlos.

In the background, they could hear Chad sobbing. "Audrey! Audrey, don't do this!"

"Ignore him, he'll be fine," said Audrey, rolling her eyes. "Jane, we're really glad to have you on the team, and you're sure you can handle Cotillion duties too?"

"For sure!" said Jane.

"Great," said Audrey, and she dumped the box on Jane. "That's all the planning we've done so far. You're going to have to work closely with Mal, since it's her big debut. Although hold on, I don't think Ben's asked her yet, so she probably has no idea she has to do all this. So maybe remind Ben he's got to formally ask her."

"He's working on it as we speak," said Jane.

Audrey didn't respond, and tapped her pen against her forehead, thinking. "What else. Oh, and do you have a date yet? Just curious."

"No," said Jane. "Not yet."

Carlos blushed and tried to look somewhere else. He'd heard vaguely about Cotillion, but hadn't realized that it was a date type of situation. So far at all the balls and parties, everyone went as a group, even Mal and Ben.

"Oh," said Audrey, looking condescendingly at Jane. "It's okay if you don't."

"I know it's okay," said Jane, rolling her eyes and struggling under the weight of the box. "Carlos?"

"Yes!" he said hopefully, standing at attention.

"Will you help me bring this box back to my dorm?" she asked sweetly.

That was so not what he expected to hear, and Carlos's smile wavered a little. But he rallied. "Of course!"

Jane doesn't have a date for Cotillion.

One day at a time, he thought.

chapter
39

Oh Captain, My Captain

It was the afternoon of the final R.O.A.R. tryouts. Carlos had already won his spot on the team, and now it was Jay's turn. The field was whittled down to the last four guys, and Jay crushed them all in quick succession. If he did well in the final round, he would make the cut too.

"Ready?" said Chad, suiting up.

"Believe it," said Jay, examining his sword.

"We'll see," Chad said with a smirk, but he didn't have his usual overconfident tone and his curls appeared a tad wilted.

"Something wrong, man?" asked Jay.

Chad shrugged. "Nothing. Audrey dumped me. What-ever."

"Oh, that's too bad," said Jay. "Sorry about that."

"It just doesn't make any sense!" wailed Chad, adjusting his face mask.

The coach blew his whistle to start the match. Chad tapped his sword against Jay's. "Let's go!"

"En garde!" said the referee. *"Prets. Allez!"* On guard. Ready. Go.

"Allez," said Jay, pulling down his face mask. He raised his sword as Chad did the same. On the balcony circling the courtyard, a group of cheerleaders and random students gathered to watch the match.

Chad came out swinging, literally, and Jay feinted and parried, advanced and attacked. If the breakup with Audrey had affected Chad, he didn't show it. Years of lessons had turned him into a graceful and formidable swordsman. But Jay held his ground, executing riposte after riposte.

"You've gotten better," said Chad. "But not good enough."

Jay snorted. Chad moved left, seeing an opening, and Jay feinted right. But at the very last moment, he struck toward the left, his sword coming up underneath Chad's chin in a decisive victory. "Touché!" Jay called triumphantly, breathing hard from exertion.

The whistle blew, signaling the end of the match.

Chad removed his face mask in annoyance. "You cheated!"

Jay hesitated, but the coach was clapping his hands, and there were cheers from the balcony. Jay looked up and saluted Mal, Evie, and Carlos, who had come to support him.

"It's a legal move," said the coach. "He won fair and square. Good job, Jay. Welcome to R.O.A.R."

Chad threw his sword and shield down on the mat in disgust.

"Thanks," said Jay, grinning widely.

"You beat the captain of the team," said the coach.

"Chad was captain?"

"Not anymore," said the coach. "Now you are."

Chad stormed off in agony. He'd lost his pride and his captaincy all in one fell swoop.

"Good job," said Lonnie, who'd been watching from the balcony.

"Thanks," said Jay, pleased with how everything had turned out. He smiled when he realized he hadn't even had to steal anything to get what he wanted. He'd done it all by playing by the rules.

chapter
40

Evie's 4 Hearts

"Turn around, let me see it twirl," said Evie, as Arabella stood in the middle of the room in her Cotillion dress. Arabella spun, and the dress floated gracefully around her ankles.

"It's gorgeous!"

"You're gorgeous in it," said Evie, and she took a few pins, adjusted the pleats on the neckline, and fluffed the sleeves.

The dress was an exact replica of Ariel's dress, a pale lavender color with silver accents, but with a few Evie touches—brocade instead of plain silk, a few more layers of taffeta to accentuate the waist, and lace instead of satin ribbon around the sleeves.

Arabella was back to her old fun self now that the trident had been returned to the museum, and her grandfather had no inkling of the danger she had brought to the kingdom. "What are you wearing to Cotillion?" she asked, still admiring herself in the mirror.

"I haven't even started on my dress," said Evie. "I haven't had any time for myself, I've had so many orders to fulfill for all the other events coming up first."

"How did you learn to sew so well?" asked Arabella, as she removed the garment and changed into her jeans and T-shirt.

"Back on the Isle," said Evie, putting Arabella's dress in a garment bag and zipping it up, "I was castle-schooled. I spent a lot of time at home, and I had to amuse myself."

"The Isle of the Lost must have been good for something, then," said Arabella with a smile.

"Yeah, I guess it was," said Evie. "I'm never going back, though."

"Of course not." Arabella shuddered. "Who would ever want to go back there?"

Evie nodded. The past was past, and it was time to concentrate on what the future would bring. She escorted Evie out of the door just as it opened again.

"Hi-ho," said Doug, who'd shown up to take her to dinner.

"Hey, Doug." She gave him an affectionate hug. "I'll be ready in a sec, I just have to make a few more adjustments to this dress," she said, taking out the beautiful blue-and-gold dress that she'd hidden from Arabella.

Doug took a seat at her desk and saw all the messy receipts, calculations, and dress orders. "Is this how you're keeping track of all your clients?" he asked.

Evie glanced over and looked embarrassed. "I've been meaning to get organized, I just haven't had time. Orders keep piling up, and I need all my free time to sew."

"Here, let me do it," said Doug, taking his laptop out of his backpack. "I'll make a spreadsheet and keep track of payments."

"You will?" she asked.

"Yeah, dwarfs are really good accountants. We have to be, with all the diamonds and jewels in the mine," he explained.

"That would be such a great help!" she enthused, watching as he began to plug numbers into a column.

They worked side by side for a moment, Evie on the dress and Doug filing away all the order slips. When he was done he showed her the invoicing system he'd set up. "So you just enter the name here, and then the dress here, and the amount here," he explained.

"You are a lifesaver!" she said. "Oh, and I came up with a name for my label."

"Yeah?"

"Evie's 4 Hearts. You like it?" she asked. "I got it from

Mal's spell. You know, the one that says 'The Power of Four Hearts Are Better than One.'"

Doug smiled. "I love it."

Evie sat back down at her sewing machine. Doug watched her thread a needle. "Oh, and Evie?" he said finally.

"Yes?" she asked, the needle in her teeth.

"I've been meaning to ask, will you be my date for Cotillion?" he said nervously.

"Me?" she said coyly.

"Um, I don't see any other princesses in the room?" he said. "Unless you'd rather go with a prince?" His shoulders slumped.

"Why would I do that when I have you?" Evie said warmly. "Of course I'll be your date. I'm honored. I was wondering when you would ask me, actually."

Doug mopped his forehead in relief. "I still can't believe you're real, that we're real. It's like a fairy tale."

"Fairy tales come true," said Evie with her sweetest smile.

"By the way, where were you guys?" asked Doug. "I was looking all over for you the other day."

Evie put away the dress and grabbed her purse. "Oh, let's just say we had a little excitement under the sea. But we've got to hurry. Ben wants us all there in five minutes. So I'll tell you all about it at dinner."

"Great. Oh, and I wanted to warn you, we're eating with

my dad and Uncle Sneezy tonight. I'll try and make sure you're not sitting next to him."

"Does he always have a cold?" asked Evie wonderingly.

"Allergies," said Doug.

chapter

41

A Second Chance to Make a First Impression

Mal's final class of the day was her favorite: Freestyle Painting, where she could do whatever she wanted. She was looking forward to working on her self-portrait, which covered an entire wall in the studio. When Mal turned the corner, she was surprised to find the classroom not only empty of other students and the usual mess of paints and canvases, but also sparkling clean and overwhelmed with dozens of flower arrangements.

"Um, what is happening?" she said, just as Ben stepped out from behind a garland.

"Mal," he said, taking her hand with a look of adoration

in his eyes. "Remember I wanted to ask you something?"

"Sort of?" she said, not quite sure what was happening, as her heart began to pound painfully in her chest. But as she glanced around the room, she got a better look at the flowers. It was sweet of him to have remembered that her favorites were black dahlias and bat orchids. The room was bursting with their sweet-but-spicy scents.

"Mal, will you be my lady at Cotillion?" he asked.

She looked at Ben. "Um, okay?" she said. Ben looked so sweet and sincere kneeling before her, and of course she would do whatever he needed her to do.

"Great!" he said, folding her into his arms.

Mal smiled, looking deep into his eyes, just as hundreds of balloons fell from the ceiling and the paparazzi came out of their hiding places, dozens of cameras flashing.

"Ben, I'm so sorry, I tried to keep it a secret, but they followed you guys in here," said Jane, wringing her hands.

"It's all right," said Ben. "I'm sorry they're here. I wanted this just to be our moment," he added to Mal.

"It's okay. You're the king. Everyone wants to know what's going on with your life," Mal said, glad that she had changed out of her torn jeans and leather jacket and worn a cute dress that Evie had loaned her as part of the beginning of her makeover.

"Oh!" she said, shielding her eyes from the glare of the flashes. She tried to pose prettily.

"Hooray!" said Evie, rushing out to give Mal a hug, followed by Jay and Carlos, who were holding even more flowers. Jane appeared to have begun berating one of the journalists in attendance.

Mal smiled at all of them, feeling as if she had just won something that she didn't quite ask for. Ben pulled her into a hug and she whispered in his ear, "By the way, what's Cotillion?"

"It's a dance," said Ben, waving to the cameras with kingly grace. "You get introduced to the kingdom and officially become Lady Mal."

Ben looked completely happy, but now it was Mal's turn to be nervous. Lady Mal? That sounded . . . fancy and serious. She'd never had a title before. Unless you counted Mal the Worst, which is what she'd been called back on the Isle of the Lost. There were so many ways to be wicked; she could dream up so many if she tried. . . .

"Oh," she said again. "When is it?"

"Soon, but there are all these events leading up to it first, sort of wrapped up with the Celebration of Auradon. We're going to tour the kingdom, make sure you meet all our subjects," said Ben.

Mal gritted her teeth in determination. She could do it. She would be perfect from this day forward, all the way up to Cotillion. She would play the part of royal girlfriend to the hilt. "Ben, can I ask you something?" she said.

"Sure. Anything," he said, kissing her hand.

"Can I move my mom out of the library and into my room? I don't think she's a threat to the kingdom as a lizard."

Ben thought about it and smiled. "Yeah, I think that can be arranged."

"Thanks, Ben."

Mal took a deep breath. Cotillion was not too far away, plus she had all those Celebration of Auradon events to accompany Ben to. Agrabah's festival was next on the calendar, so a royal visit to Aladdin and Jasmine was in the works. She was going to do her best, she promised herself, thinking of the spell book temporarily hidden back in her dorm room.

She just had to make a few changes here and there. . . .

chapter

42

The Villains of Our Story

Uma, Harry, and Gil stood on the deck of the shipwrecked *Lost Revenge*. Their clothes were almost dry from the storm, and they were no worse for wear. But the ship was another story altogether. The mainmast was broken, there were holes in the hull, and it was clear she would never sail again. She would be a permanent addition to the dock from now on. The three of them leaned over the railing on the topmost deck, watching the colorful, messy lives of pirates and villains unfold in the rickety wooden tenements right across from the bridge.

Uma stared moodily at the lively scene in front of her without seeing anything. She still couldn't understand what had happened out there on the Isle of the Doomed. She definitely swam down to the ocean floor and grabbed the trident—that was a memory, not a dream, she was sure. But how was it that she had ended up back on the rowboat without the trident, using her mother's necklace to call it up? And why had she lost to Mal, of all people? Mal, who wasn't even a proper villain anymore, but an Auradon turncoat. Mal, who wasn't worthy of her mother's name, let alone her legacy. Mal, who had gone soft and was dating the king of Auradon—gross. Mal, who'd beaten her once again.

It was way too painful to dwell upon, so Uma decided she'd been robbed, not beaten. That trident had been rightfully hers, but Mal had done something, used some horrible Auradon magic, and cheated Uma out of her victory.

"So what now?" asked Gil.

"Rough up goblins?" suggested Harry.

"Ooh, or taunt first-years and make them walk the plank!" said Gil.

"Uma?" asked Harry. "Captain's choice?"

She shook herself out of her reverie. She still had Mal's glove in her pocket, but she planned on burning it in the kitchen fire soon enough. "I've got a better idea," said Uma.

She led them out across the bridge and into the bazaar. The stalls were full of hawkers, and she and her pirates had a fun time swiping scarves, taking things that weren't theirs, and causing the usual chaos and mayhem.

"Look," she said, stopping in front of a puke-inducing poster of King Ben and Mal. "Spray paint," she ordered, holding out a palm, and Harry slapped a canister in her hand.

"Let's give him a nice little mustache and horns, shall we?" she said, drawing them over Ben's head and face.

The pirates snickered. "There's more over there," said Gil.

The crew vandalized every poster of King Ben that they could find, especially ones that depicted him and that Isle traitor Mal. It was a petty victory, but it did make Uma feel better, especially when she scrawled the pirates' motto all over their faces: *WE RIDE WITH THE TIDE.*

Uma examined her handiwork with a smile. Once she was satisfied that there wasn't a poster of the king that wasn't defaced on the Isle of the Lost, they headed back to their ship.

"Still, it's too bad we lost," said Gil, leaning back on the railing with a frown. They were facing the other way now, looking out into the ocean at Auradon in the distance.

"Lost? We didn't lose!" said Uma. "We never lose!"

But Harry's sly pirate's face burst into a grin. "Exactly! We never really had a chance anyway!"

"Huh?" Gil looked confused, but Uma had an inkling of what Harry was trying to say.

Harry's smile grew wider. "Come on. We're trapped here. Look up there!" he said, pointing to the sky. "That invisible barrier? It's impossible to get off the Isle of the Lost. The deck was stacked against us from the beginning."

Uma raised her fist to the sky in annoyance. Harry was right. They were playing long odds, betting against the house, and the house always wins. She knew that, since she and Harry ran a dice game at the fish shop every other Thursday.

"Listen, we might not have the trident, and we might not have a way off this island," said Harry. "But we've got a serious crew here."

Uma looked around at the pirates on the ship—Desiree, Jonas, Bonny, even Gonzo. They were hers. A real crew.

"We've got a lot to do," said Harry. "So much trouble to start, eh?" He slung an arm around Uma, and another around Gil.

"Ugh," said Gil. "You smell like shrimp."

"Um, that's me," said Uma.

"No, it's me," said Harry with a wiggle of his eyebrows. "I just had breakfast."

But the three of them stood there for a bit, with their arms over each other's shoulders, looking out to the ocean and to the distant skyline of Auradon. Because Harry was right. They might not have much, but they were each part of a pirate crew. And on the Isle of the Lost, that was more than something—it was everything.

"One day, when those Bore-a-don snobs least expect it, we'll pounce," promised Harry. "They'll make a mistake, maybe even wander into the wrong neighborhood. Fall into our net! And you know what we'll do then!" he said, making a slashing motion across his neck with his hook.

"Um, what will we do?" wondered Gil.

"We'll have our revenge," Uma declared, her eyes glittering with malice. "Mark my words. This isn't the end of our story. It's only the beginning."

TO FIND OUT WHAT HAPPENS NEXT . . .

Premieres Summer 2017

acknowledgments

As ever, a huge, heartfelt, sliding-in-right-before-the-deadline thank you of gratitude and relief to my main peeps who help make these books happen: my editors Julie Rosenberg and Emily Meehan, my publicist Seale Ballenger, and our faithful compatriots at Disney Channel: Naketha Mattocks and Carin Davis. Thanks for believing!

Thank you to everyone at Disney Publishing and Disney Channel including Andrew Sugerman, Raj Murari, Mary Ann Naples, Gary Marsh, Jennifer Rogers-Doyle, Adam Bonnett, Laura Burns, Kate Reagan, Hannah Allaman, Mary Ann "MAZ!" Zissimos, Elena Blanco, Kim Knueppel, Sarah Sullivan, Jackie De Leo, Frank (Frankie BOOM!) Bumbalo, Dina Sherman, Elke Villa, Andrew Sansone, Holly Nagel, Alex Eiserloh, Maggie Penn, Sadie Hillier, Marybeth Tregarthen, Sara Liebling, Guy Cunningham,

Dan Kaufman, David Jaffe, Meredith Jones, Marci Senders, James Madsen, and Russ Gray.

Thank you to the talented stars of *Descendants 2* who are so inspiring and always fun to watch—Dove Cameron, Sofia Carson, Cameron Boyce, Booboo Stewart, Mitchell Hope, Brenna D'Amico, Dianne Doan, Jedidiah Goodacre, Zachary Gibson, and the awesome new pirates China McClain, Thomas Doherty, and Dylan Playfair.

Thank you, Kenny Ortega, for making another fun movie!

Thank you to Richard Abate, Rachel Kim, and everyone at 3Arts. Thank you, Talia Hurst and Candy Ford for everything you do at home to keep it running.

Thank you to my family—Mom, Steve, Aina, Nicholas, and Joseph Green; Chito, Christina, Sebastian, and Marie de la Cruz, Terence, Trina, and Olivia Lim; Odette and Christina Gaisano; Clarke, Isabel and, Cailyn Ng; Sony and Badong Torre; Melanie, Maj, and Mica Ong/Calangi, and everyone in the extended DLC-Ong clan!

Thanks to Marg and Raf always.

Big love and thanks to the YallCrew: Shane Pangburn, Tori Hill, Spencer Richardson, Jonathan Sanchez, Tahereh Mafi, Ransom Riggs, Marie Lu, Kami Garcia, Brendan Reichs, Sandy London, Veronica Roth, Holly Goldberg Sloan, Patrick Dolan, and Emily Williams.

Thank you my CH crew: Heidi and Andy McKenna, Jill Lorie and Steve Stewart, Cole Hartman, Tiffany Moon,

Dan and Dawn Limerick, Carol Koh and Tony Evans, Sean Curley and Bronwyn Savasta, Gloria Jolley and Scott Johnson, Fatima Goncalves and Auggie Ruiz, Mike and Betty Balian, Saher and Bassil Hamideh, Ava and Ron McKay, Nicole and Chris Jones, Bob and Carolyn Holmes, Celeste and Patrick Vos, Jenni and Adam Gerber, and Molly and Chad Ludwig.

Huge thanks to all the rotten little Descenders!

Thanks most to everyone on our Netflix account: especially Mike, who stopped working on his book to help with mine, Mattie, the light of our lives, Mimi, loyal hound, and Summer, who's still alive (she's a beta). Mama can hang out again.